URBAN GRIST
WRITTEN BY TOM PR

CW01499320

THE BASTARD WOULD LIKE TO THANK

Andrea Threapleton, Mikey Robson, Michael Dailey, Stuart Place,
Julian Socha, Aiden Garbutt, Nick and Mandy Kirby Briggs,
John Mathers, Lou Mott, David Sowden, John F Keenan,
John Otway, Jade Leigh Blakeley, Giles Winterton,
Mike Jolly, Dave Knowlson, Elizabeth Crossley,
Joe Nodus, Paul Holdiay, Beth Kilburn,
 Luke and Radka Ballantyne,
Scott Doonican, Pocketful O' Nowt, Andie Mills,
 Dave Procter, Nicky Bray, Martin Trippet, Ian Bellwood,
Rosalind Evans and anyone else whose had me
up and had to suffer listening to me read this shit.

Trust me, it sounds better on the page.

MERCHANDISED

Rolling Stones tour of the US
Dated 1978
Worn with an ambivalence
That makes me wanna gip
I doubt you were there
You've barely got any pubic hair
You wear the colours
That signify another
Who've actually taken the time
To listen to the chimes
Of the restless hearts
That struggled to start
That lost direction
On sex N Drugs N sausage rolls
Trend shouldn't be an ambition
You posing arsehole
Flying the flag
Distracted by the only hit
From a band
That you secretly think are shit
As you wait to be recognised
By those that realised
That true music is a way of life
And not just a market strategized
For liable stillborns
Who live on one fucking song
That Heart F.M
Chooses to display now N again
I hate to be blunt
But you're a fucking cunt
With your hipster agenda
That holds no closure
I don't think your cool
I don't think your hip
You're about as interesting
As a urinary drip
Take the time
And listen to the band

That you advertise
With your immature idealistic stand
If not, then stay in the shopping centre
Keep your pulse on the fashion line
Get back with the sheep
And perish with the rest of the merchandised

TEMPORARY POSITION

A walking talking hairpiece
Asks me where I wanna be in five years
With his Primark suit
And fetish for targets
Would I be interested
In a supervisor position?
Thanks but no thanks
I don't fancy been a babysitter
I can't climb up the ladder
Cos I have a thing about heights
I just wanna get paid, get drunk
Cos that's how I like to spend my nights
I'm not interested in team work
Cos I'm here for myself
I'll stay before the rot sets in
Cos it's a threat to my health
I'll work at my own pace
And go for a wank in the bogs
I'm easily bored
And I always need a smoke
Don't ask me to do overtime
Cos I don't wanna be here in the first place
I'll do what I can
Until I'm comfortably replaced
By some hipster student
Who thinks everything's a laugh
There's nothing fun sweating for eight hours
You useless twat
I'm your worst enemy
Who on paper seems exact
To act nicey nicey
Then slag you off behind your back
I'm asked to give an example
On superior customer service
It must've been when I phone in sick
And had a marathon of acid trips
You ask me why I'm the best person
For the applied job

Cos I fucking showed up
You stupid sod
Am I analytical?
Can I work under pressure?
I can barely get out of bed
Let alone think of a good answer
To your double handed query
You ask with smug eloquence
If I could earn a living picking my arse
Then I'd certainly take the chance
You want me to describe myself
And to be specific
But I'm just another burnout
You pretentious prick
You need to know
Why I'm in the job market
Cos I need the money
To settle my local's debt
You ask me what I'm looking for
As if I'm Bono from U2
I obviously haven't found it
So that's why I'm talking to you
I'm not here for the long run
My objectives are short
No sweat off my arse if I'm selected or not
Cos I don't fancy been bought
Just another stand in
Another job seeking orphan
Life is a temporary position
And we're always here to go

SNIDE

I'm just minding my own business
What's wrong with that?
We've only just met
But I can tell you're a twat
I can't walk the street
Without been pressured
For a generous donation
And a pint of blood
No I don't have a spare cig
Thirty grams dunt last a week anymore
I just used up my last 30p
In a phone box to be retro
Excuse me I must be going
To wherever you're not
My weekends are for staying indoors
Cursing whatever I haven't got
I don't take kindly to threats
From a bloke whose trousers are around his knees
Wipe the mother's milk from your gob
And learn to stand up when you pee
You pull a nice wheelie
Now turn round and get to fuck
No point in taking the high road and been polite
Cos you end up bombarded by insults
I'm told if I'm seen again
I'll be knocked down where I stand
What? In your playmobil car!
You maladjusted, brain damaged bag of wank
Suddenly I'm approached by a bloke named Quill
Who says he's willing to take a dare
I tell him I'm an undercover copper
And then watch him fade into vaporised air
Then walks up Fagan with broken teeth
Hoping I'll put me bank details in his cup
But I mumble an apology N walk away
Only to be told I'm a cunt
I'm just as desperate as you
But I prefer to keep it under wraps

Don't blame me if the benefits don't fit
And the fountain of youth's turned flat
I'm your enemy
Cos I'm in the wrong place
What you've forgotten
Is that we're all the same
In this shit hole
In which we hide
We call it home
As our existence slides
Keep your mouth shut
And pass me by
You never know who you're gonna meet
So don't be so snide

INEBRIATED

I just wanna get drunk
I just wanna get high
Not have to worry
About the days moving by
I don't care about solutions
To the problems in my mind
I just wanna absolution
At the end of the day's grind
Refill my glass
Roll that number
Cut that line
I want to be dumber
Don't tell me of your problems
Cos I don't give a toss
I just wanna slant
Into an elusive moss
That pollutes my brain cells
And makes my heart sink
Don't fuck about
Pour me another drink
This lucid apathy
Makes me a friend to the earth
Hardwired N suffocating
On discount turf
Smoked with derision
In the movie set car park
With dreamy situations
That alight in the dark
I don't care about tomorrow
Cos it always comes around
Light my cigarette
And I'll be sound as a pound
Forget about substance
It's just a cliché
I like the dark bars
For their social decay
Don't tell me to take it eazee
I've been doing that all my life

That's why I've got a chip on both shoulders
And I'm overcome with strife
Crack open another dream can
And well talk this out
Pay for another round
So we can understand what it's all about
I puke in the gutter
But I'm doing just fine
The watering holes have dried up
But we've got plenty of time
I wanna be ambiguous
Capricious and celebratory
Sink a drink N be dangerous
In numbed civility
I don't wanna remember yesterday
It plays too much on my mind
Let's forget about today
It was shit so let's have a pint
Let's set up in the park
But keep an eye out for the cops
We'll fill up the beer cuts
And then pop to the all night shop
When the bottle reaches its end
When we reach the last dreg
When the money runs out
We'll go back home instead
For a three-day party
Another weekly bender
Our daily sense is to lose control
That is our main agenda
No time for eloquence
I don't care if I'm a disgrace
I just wanna cancel my subscription
To the human race
Gimme another snifter
Let's have another dram
I've got work in the morning
But I don't give a damn
Don't worry bout me
I'm just getting shit faced

Out of control N inebriated
Is my safe place

THE DAY I TOOK OFF WORK

I was out hunting Wolverine's
I travelled in a yellow Submarine
I was in Narnia attending a party
Ferris Bueller's got nothing on me
The day I took off work

I won the lottery several times in a row
Bought a motorboat and a stately home
Invested in Marmite N Toblerone (For some reason)
Placed a bet N then lost it all
The day I took off work

I saved the world from an alien invasion
Then discovered the key to matching socks
I managed to cure all of my trepidations
Then discovered Madeline McCann in a jack in the box
The day I took off work

Racing through minefields
Navigating through asteroids
I administered a marriage
Between a cowboy N his horse
Who're now on their honeymoon
They sent me a postcard
The day I took off work
Was one continuous mardi gras

I built a time machine out of a fridge
I helped Led Zeppelin write a comeback hit
I aided Force 10 in blowing up that damn bridge
And managed to make Lego and Megablox pieces fit
The day I took off work

I tripped the light fantastic
And burnt the candle at both ends
Partying from dusk til dawn
Until the glow sent me round the bend
The day I took off work

I awoke in an alternative universe
Where Cobain and Ian Curtis never hailed that hearse
Where a red light means Go and a green light means reverse
Tell me sir does this sound too absurd
When I tell you what I did on me day off?

With a twist N shout
I restored Atlantis
I got the ark of the covenant
Back from the Nazi's
I flew around the sun
And mastered running in slow motion
The day I took off work
Was filled with commotion
Life is a dream
And that says it all
The day I took off work
Was a splendiferous, manic, unbelievable fucking bore!

SHIT THAT KEEPS ME AWAKE AT NIGHT

I wonder if on Predator's planet
There's a band called 'The Ugly Motherfuckers'
I lie awake in bed wondering if
Kaiser Sose will ever be captured
When will somebody tell Vicky Patterson
That nobody gives a shit?
Will Richard Hammond finally perish
In one of his many 'accidents'?
When will that ginger cow
Stop asking me if I wanna bingo?
and is origami in fact a genuine martial art
Cos I don't know
I wonder
How much wood could a woodchuck chuck if a woodchuck could
chuck wood
I like to imagine that Godot finally arrived
And that Donny from the Big Lebowski will finally shut the fuck up

Did John Lennon really burn down that house
After his affair like in the song Norwegian Wood?
Cos I'd really like to find out
Others worry about Brexit
But this is the shit that keeps me awake at night

When will people realize
That Howard the Duck is a good movie?
Could I physically achieve a handstand
The next time I go for a pee?
I need answers to these questions
To be rid of this insomnia
I lost all my faith in the magic eight ball
When it kept giving me the same answers
I wonder if that whore
Was kind enough to keep Van Gough's ear
There are so many mysteries
That I would like to be made clear
But the one thing that bothers me
And will most likely plague until I'm old

Is who shot first
Han Solo or Greedo?

Will I spontaneously combust
If I fart, burp N sneeze
At the same time?
I'm haunted by these
Internal enquiries
This is the shit that keeps me awake at night

YOU'RE NEVER ALONE WITH A HAND

When you're in the mood
But she's not broody
Don't get upset
Have a five finger party
When you're overcome with passion
But she's on the rag
And not wooed by your proposition
That you'll go round the back
Just cradle your balls
And work the shaft
Cos you're never alone with a hand

When you're on a dry spell
And not had any for months
And the horizontal disco
Won't ease those 'headaches' of hers
Lower your blood pressure twice a day
Keep your hand in a bag of rice
Get your kicks your own way
To ease those lonely nights
Go on a crusade of self-harm
Cos you're never alone with a hand

Become a renowned lover
Of your own practice
Face off the one armed man
With a wrist of elastic
Don't sit there broken hearted
When she spurns your advances
Just check the door before you molest yourself
To avoid any embarrassment
Become inseparable with your palm
Cos you're never alone with a hand

Any woman could be yours
Any dog would fetch
But when you're on your tod
Grabbing the devil by the horns works out best

Nobody knows better
Nobody touches YOU like yourself
Train that iron grip of yours
For the betterment of your health
Spend some time with your favourite gland
Cos you're never alone with a hand

BANG YOUR HEAD AGAINST THE WALL

My head is filled
With nasty shit
Like dirt in the fingernails
That never fucking shifts
I can't pontificate
You wouldn't understand
I don't wanna talk
I just wanna suspend
The nagging doubts
And nervous exhaustion
That makes me wish
I was a product of abortion
I have a drink
And my mind goes sideways
I have a smoke
And the day runs away
A sly remark from the boss born last week
Makes me see red
The shop doesn't have amber leaf
So I'm stuck with Golden Grief instead
5 cans of Oranjeboom
On the back of the bus
Same thing all the time
Leaves you fucking fed up
No rizlas
So I roll a number in the ticket
The taste of ink on my tongue
Stops me from breathing
Two-day release
From my contracted sentence
Then back to absurdity
Devoid of common sense
Stuck at home
Tied up in knots
Not economically viable
Every application is bankrupt
Just a fabricated fabrication
Of askew reality

A temporary position
That takes an eternity
The same old shit
With the same outcome
I'm banging my head against the wall
Under modern slavery's boredom

URGENT APPEAL

This is an urgent appeal
For the men N women
Lumbered with a shitty deal
Pot less from the price of admission

Who never had the right to choose
Whether they would win or lose
As soon as they left school
Lost in the vocation queue

This is an urgent appeal
For the boy's N girls
Who can't afford to steal
The benefits N the perks

Awake in the broken system
No clue, no ambition
Trapped in the cistern
Of their private prisons where nobody listens

This is an urgent appeal
To the lives assigned
To moments unreal
In the sickness of the mind

WISHING THE DAYS AWAY

Ten hours
Then I'm out the door
To read the boards I've walked before
Ten hours
Pinned to the hands
The final straw looming to strike me down
Every party comes to a halt
But the yearning always remains intact
All the time looking for a good time
Intent to never come back
Ten hours
Until my blue haven shields me
From the interest to survive
Ten hours
On the conveyer belt
Until I forget that I'm alive
Swimming in the sorrows
Content to drown my mind
Dancing in the shadows
Waltzing with the left behinds
Ten hours
Then I can do one
Thinking of plans I quickly abort
Ten hours
Agonising in the eternal merry go round
Arriving as quick as a change of heart
Collecting crumbs in the slumber
Through the continuity of the continuous
The globe wheezing to a dead halt
As another day appears to consume us
Ten hours
Under cancerous bulbs
Stumbling in headless circles
Ten hours
Within the still seconds
As the moments dodge and the days hurtles
Catching up to lost time
That quickly evaporates

There's nothing worth saying
I'm just wishing the days away

DEAD INSIDE

Annoying
Incomprehensible
BMX warrior
About seven
Years old
Says
I better watch
Where I'm walking
And how I shouldn't be so bold
Obscenities
Uttered haphazardly
Spat from
Inflated
Gums
As he
Hollers
In pre –
Pubescent
Outrage
Expressive N dumb
Like
Disturbing
A felines territory
Through the garages
On the
Edge of
The abandoned dimension
Like a
Stagehand
Wandering into
Focus
In the scenic soap opera
I knock
The chain
On his bike
And watch
Him drop
Into the foetal position

Do you think I need this?
When I'm distracted by daily errands
I just wanna get there and get gone
Before my uncomfortability extends
I cannot lie
There's nothing left to take
I'm dead inside
So leave me alone for Christ sake

Vicious
Personal space invaders
Demanding
I empty me pockets
Because
A
Good deed
For a friend
Unseen
Will
Leave
Me in
God's favour
As
If
Charity
Is something to boast
An
Imprint
On the skyscraper
Of existence
But
I'm
Flat broke
And
Tired
Of the
Insistence
And
The need

To bleed
For other
People's
Opinions of me

Do you think I need this?
When I'm distracted by daily errands
I just wanna get there and get gone
Before my uncomfortability extends
I cannot lie
There's nothing left to take
I'm dead inside
So leave me alone for Christ sake

Attentive
Socially active
Priestess
Of
The
Redundant
Stops me
In
My
Ruthless
Stride
To ask
Why I
Look
So down
Telling
Me
There
Is more
Energy in
Sadness
And
That
I
Should
Take

The time
To smile

Do you think I wear black
Cos I'm a cheery character?
Do you think the reason I don't smile
Is cos I'm complying to some typical apparel?
I hate to be cruel
But you give me no choice
Now ride off
On your lame horse
I cannot tell a lie
There's nothing left to take
I'm dead inside
Now leave me alone for fuck sake

FREE PINT MERCERNARY

He's back at the local
Throat as dry as a boot
Rough as a butchers arse
With no currency to lose
No cash to burn
Shakes in his digits
With his mood on the turn
Overfed on greasy ashtray biscuits
The barmaids give him dirty looks
The fixtures think he's hustling for coins
The bouncers all place their bets
As the game is on point
Smooth entry on the Westside of the crooked pool table
Between the two gents wearing the same shirt
As he makes a clean path to the beer garden
Dodging the weekend philosophers as he downs the dregs left by the
world cup thugs
Ten down as he makes his way into the pit
As a bird gets elbowed trying to take her empty glass to the bar
Athletic energy with elastic feet as the bloke with the stupid haircut
Gets tackled trying to take out his yellow card
He swipes number thirty from the jukebox abuser
Wide eyed and pissed after two pints of Carlsberg
As he slips inside the services only to find blown up jonnies
And an unflushable depth charge laughing in the bog
Bombarded by insults
That he takes in his stride
He gets to the halfway point
To find the place has died
The local heroes are comatose
The stools are on the table
The bouncers lock up the doors
And the staff are no longer available
Ashe lunges towards the optics
A night cap nice N neat
As the bouncers grab him N say: "Try again tomorrow"
And throw him out into the street

LS12 BOY

By the five towers
Along the winker green
Through imperial terrace
Up to far fold lane
With the tall tales
And Mecca Bingo dreams
They want flat beer
And second hand jeans
Take me down the road
To your brother's flat
For some powdered wisdom
In a see through bag
Tell me all your jokes
Though I've heard them all
You claim the North will rise
When the West shall fall
Where the kisses are counterfeit
And the night has a thousand black eyes
Where the drugs don't work
Where the only rule is to survive
It's written on the wind
And the stolen number plates
It's whispered in the nights
That never leave a trace

All dressed up
Just to stay put
A one in a million LS12 Boy
Stuck on hesitation row

Murmured pulses
And bathroom cocktails
On the street of abandoned artists
With fully furnished cells
Gimme ashtray sonnets
And Westway psychos
In the sofa linings
Where nobody goes

I like your T-shirt
Though you haven't heard the songs
By the merchandised
You spent all your money on
Devilishly charismatic
Like a packet of crisps
On a lifelong quest
To find the plural of sheep
Where tokens of love are death sentences
Where friendliness is treated like a hate crime
Technicolour dreams become monochrome nightmares
As all the clocks lose their sense of time
It's plastered on the walls
In the one star accommodations
Where hatred is infinite
And love is conditioned

All dressed up
Just to stay put
A one in a million LS12 Boy
Stuck on hesitation row

I DON'T WANNA BE WELL

Gimme lean cuisine heart disease
I wanna be stuck with industrial pleurisy
Brewers droop and smokers cough
With a void where my immune system used to be
Book me a holiday in a hospital bed
Until I'm fit for work
Save my coma for the weekend
With severed veins and fractured nerves

Don't gimme the cure
I operate on internal dysfunction
I don't wanna be well
Just medicate me on proletariat pollution

Gimme detox jitters in my sticky fingers
Street scene mobility scooter drag races
Black hydro carbonated barnacles on my stuttering lungs
Overwhelmed by conditions that become diseases
Fatal haemorrhages from innocent sneezes
Coffin reservations for the change in weather
Aneurysms in natural highs
Grand mal seizures to make me feel better

Don't gimme the cure
I operate on internal dysfunction
I don't wanna be well
Just medicate me on proletariat pollution

GO THE EXTRA MILE

She's in a mood
Stay in the other room
With a white flag
As the tension grows
Wrapped up in a shit storm
Due to a lapse in form
As the minute's drag
And you become afraid to blow your own nose
Her words can kill
It's happened before
But she's more enticing
When she wants to settle the score
About something that happened
Several years in the past
Trapped in the misdirection
Of confusing your mouth with your arse
Need to get it settled
Work everything out
Even the playing field
To ease her screams N shouts
Can't go to bed angry
Cos it's just bad form
If so you'll probably be castrated
In the early morn
That delicate tongue
Filled with venom
Like a knife jabbing
At your perishable armour
The sound of broken glass
She scares the shit out of the cat
There's only worth thing trying
And that's to piss her off even more

Go the extra mile
And get the silent treatment
A nice couple of hours
Will make you feel relieved
Say something obtuse

Even obnoxious
Tell her it's not a big deal
Or call her mother a hippopotamus
Be succinct
Delicate but dishonourable
Tell her dying her moustache blonde
Won't make it any less noticeable

The only sensible outcome
To let the madness cease
To stop the aggression
And give you peace
It's a competition
Where neither is the victor
But you can calm the storm
By digging a little deeper
Stick to your guns
And play your cards right
You might get an angry shag
At the end of the night
But be careful
When crossing the fine line
For it's just an increase
For an unpayable fine

Love is a many splendored thing
Once in a while
But to shut her up
Go the extra mile

EVERYBODY WANTS SOMEONE TO KILL

You're too nice
You can't fool me
You wanna put your neighbours head in a vice
Its easy to see
Everyone has an enemy
Everyone has a foe
Names on a list
With a homemade voodoo doll

You can't bullshit a bullshitter
Don't think me naïve
At the end of the day
Everybody wants someone to kill

That bloke who overturned you
Deserves to perish in a nasty crash
That bellend who nicked the last teabag
Needs to have his cranium smashed
Don't act so pleasant
Cos I'm not fooled
Ultra violence comes to mind
When some prick ruins your mood

You can't bullshit a bullshitter
Don't think me naïve
At the end of the day
Everybody wants someone to kill

That scumbag with the obnoxious flare
Needs a shovel round the head
One fatal blow without hesitation
And he'll be dead
The mouthy git after too many pints
Needs a shotgun to the face
One squeeze of the trigger
And he's gone without a trace
You can't hide it
Where all the same

Fantasising psychotic retribution
On those we'd like to mame
It could be your best friend
Or your significant other
A long awaited stranger
That you'd gladly smother
Overfilled with blood lust
That we push down with other resentments
Hoping and praying they'll contract
Some degenerative ailment
Disguising our torment in hope of some relief
But everybody needs someone
Yes, everybody wants someone
Everybody needs someone to kill

CASSANEVER

I'm the box you can't think outside of
Would you like to go back to your place with me?
Here comes the Cassanever on a curfew
His mums his roommate and they get along famously

He's got the sweet talk
Tainted with a rapist wit
Comes off
Like a desperate tit
She's not interested mate
Take my word for it
He says his loves like diarrhoea
And that he can't keep it in
Telling her she heals quickly
For someone that's just fell from Heaven
Getting sexcited
At the freemans catalogue
Filled with girls in their lingerie
That he tucks behind the bog
He's got the gab
Of a tongue tied adolescent
Kicks her heels N spills his drink
So she noticrs his presence
But she's got her eyes
On the pint pulling gent
With the nice smile and probably a car
Not a high pitched voice and a motorised go kart

They say nice guys don't stand a chance
And that bastards get in first
Another Cassanever suited N booted
Out for a cook, a friend N a whore in one swerve

CORNERSHOP MAFIA

Anarchist mardi gras before the street lights illuminate
Auto destructive art in the smashed up phone booth
Insults in pre-pubescent whispers
Ten deck of Mayfair and a can of strongbow
Permanent marker odes of love scratched on rusted shutters
Five aside Dullball with the automatic door as the goal
Struggling indifference in BMX numbers
Warnings drowned out by the adolescent ego

Nowhere to go
Nothing to do
Nowhere is home
That's nothing new
Along the dungeon walkways
And purgatory estates
The cornershop mafia
State their claim

Sexual appetite in the fingers of school day affairs
Crayola statements penned on unread bus timetables
Voices of rebellion in hooded attire
Inebriated on penny sweets and candy cigarettes
Bareknuckle love taps in the ring of abandoned garages
School uniform gangs with middle finger attachments
Praying for the gullibility of strangers
To cough up a bottle of multi coloured intoxicants

Nowhere to go
Nothing to do
Nowhere is home
That's nothing new
Along the dungeon walkways
And purgatory estates
The cornershop mafia
State their claim

MERCY

Mercy is an ideal
A superstition
A moralistic endeavour
That holds no achievement
Mercy is a goal
Perpetrated by the sensitive
Murmurs vibrating
In the feedback of bereavement
Nobody wins
Nobody loses
The only thing determined
Is your participation
In the grind
And anguish
Of adulthood
That needs no contribution
That needs no analysis
That develops no scrutiny
Or expectation
Just aching finality
Mercy is a symptom of weakness
A notion spawned from detachment
Reliability rests on ones isolated
Pleas in the loneliness of empty doorways
Sentiment is to be despised
Understanding is a deluded concept
Sociability does not enlarge the receptors
It just leaves one suspect
To intimidation N maladjustment
Distance must be maintained
Just another concept
With all connections restrained
Nobody wins
Nobody loses
The only thing determined
Is your participation
In the grind
And anguish

Of adulthood
That needs no contribution
That needs no analysis
That develops no scrutiny
Or expectation
Just aching finality
Mercy is a thesis
An old fashioned idea
In this city of tiny tragedies
There is no mercy here

NOW

Maybe the asphalt moon has got you in its sights as you tour the
overfilled bars
Maybe there is a young girl intensely examining your nether regions
Maybe you wait in silence for your foetus N chips in the drive thru
in your rented car
Maybe you are hankering for a cigarette in a dark room during the
empty season

I've tasted that sweat on her cheek
I've crawled through the expensive watering holes
I've feasted on undercooked nourishment
And I've lived countless lives in empty rooms

I was there
I bought the ticket
Kept the program
Saved the memories
Plotted the next move
Waited patiently
And I am there
With you now

Maybe the bottle is at its end but you are too drunk to sleep but out
of time to procure more
Maybe you are just sat in front of your TV ready to turn out the
lights and go to work in the morning
Maybe you are in the midst of some stupendous spiritual
independence
Or maybe you are grabbing the devil by the horns while sheepishly
moaning

I have shed a tear for the last drop at 3AM
I have watched those same shows repeatedly
I have pleasured myself until dry as a bone
And I intend to do it all over again

I was there
I bought the ticket

Kept the program
Saved the memories
Plotted the next move
Waited patiently
And I am there
With you now
As lost
And lonely as you
I am there with you now
Wishing
Waiting
Hoping
For
Something to do

DAYS OF DUMBNESS

Blissful ignorance
Fulfilled emptiness
Devoid of moral integrity
Addicted to abuse
United division
Opposed on every agreement
Reversing into the future
Through nerve shattering light speed
Condemned by comfortability
Secure in the isolated
Confined to instability
Marooned in the city

Vague clarity
Entangled reliability
Detached security
Mistrusting honesty
Viscous affection
Envious adoration
Bitter empathy
Confident hesitation
Gentle violence
Soft brutality
Controlled chaos
Separated duality
Hysteria composer
Fear instigator
Weird magnate
Back street crawler

If there's beauty in madness
There is sweetness in stupidity
Roll on the days of dumbness
For another millennium

Offended by happiness
Horrified by elation
Indifferent to tragedy

And disturbing noises
Comfortable in claustrophobia
Safety netted in the bad atmosphere
At home in unsafety
Clear thinking through paranoia
Joyfulness in heartbreak
Occupied in boredom
Entertained by silence
Anger burns within the settling storm

Toxic endorphins
Loose attachments
Purchase ideals
Disgust enraptured
Uncertain epiphanies
Sideways walking
Stranger familiarity
Cross-eyed staring
Untamed routine
Routinized unpredictability
Aborted mass production
Aggressive civility
Timidly arrogant
Unrequited hatred
First rate antiques
Inaudibly translated

If there's beauty in madness
There is sweetness in stupidity
Roll on the days of dumbness
For another millennium

STRONGER THAN THE SHITSTORM

Let the games commence
Let the hunt be afoot
Let's set this fucker off
And light the fuse
Let's live to lose
Let us leave a good looking corpse
In the wake of our own suicides
When the atmosphere drops
Let the cages rattle
Let's slip through the streets to our second homes
Where life is lived with battle
And furnished with beermats
Let us fall hand in hand
Let us land gracefully
Into the mania of our smiles
That hold contingency

Let's light the cocktail
Enthused in the bottle
Of our damaged vessels
That hurtle full throttle
Into the dawn
Of the rising sun
Where we enter
Into another fortune
One of similarity
One of déjà vu
The clock ticking ominously
As hell knocks upon our door
Let's share our stories
Let's celebrate the norm
Let us overcome adversity
For together we are stronger than the shitstorm
That rains on our parade
That disrupts our delicate sensibilities
Too tough to be destroyed
By the state of debility
Let us laugh off the agony

Through the long run N short term
Demented and stubborn in survival
For together we are stronger than the shitstorm

ELASTIC RADICAL

Elastic radical
On the North side turnstile
Reverie of
Distorted contorted
Seminal vibes
Ecstatic frolic
Of the grand mal pinnacle
Influence in
Demented electric
Dawn of the new millennial
Gorilla therapist
In the downbeat concrete
Conspiracies
With uprooted N deluded
Crooked beat
Plastic maniac
Jittering itchycoo hullabaloo
In the safety
Of stale dairy
Processed in blue suede shoes
Superstitious infectious
Mission of the spellbound
Matchless insanity
An ambient transient
Stalked by hells hounds
Motion sickness princes
With graveyard fingernails
Digging deep
In the divine spines
Of the sirens wail
Savage language
In the ruptured culture
Animosity
With polythene civility
Of bulbous conjectures
Semen serums
Concocted haphazardly
To cure

Hideous intrusions
Of fugazi
Seminal hysterical
Slipshod dewdrop
Chemicals
Severing the nerves
As blood rots
Viscous carnivorous
Angels of desperation
Debating
Grievous beliefs
Of the new sensation
Dead vegetables
Serving N perverting
The hustle
Of damaged language
With exhausted muscle
Elastic radical
In the downlow undergrowth
Pleasure of
Safety in conformity
Automatically controlled

FACTORY FLOOR

I fell asleep in thorns
With metal hooked in my veins
I buttoned up my coat
As the confusion reigned
I nestled with the chancers
Stating my hopeful claim
I awoke within handcuffs
Not knowing my own name
Sustained with multi-coloured
Aphrodisiacs of the bored
I can't waste anymore time
On the factory floor

They drilled me into the system
And stole all of my details
I was instructed in repetition
Then left wayward in the remains
My blood was slowly auctioned
By the thirsty gavel pimps
Who struggled with their morality
As they handed out wage sliops
As all the high vis bouncers
Guarded every door
I can't waste anymore time
On the factory floor

I was left stranded
In language without a voice
I continued obsoletely
Without any choice
With the issue of seize the day
I lost my sonic pulse
Not known carpe diems meaning
As I clock into the hub
Running round in circles
Until I can go home
I can't waste anymore time
On the factory floor

SUPPORT YOUR LOCAL VANDALS

Concreate off a motorway bridge
Bricks through the bus stop windows
Tyres slashed on the motorway strip
Cars colliding into off licence doors
Disobey the conformity mainstream
Get a degree in subvertising
Wing mirrors for trophies
High quality culture jamming

Support your local vandals
Support the aerosol kings
Support the white van pranksters
And the artists without funding

Irregular soldiers ignite the petrol bomb
Hoping to tag everything in sight
Trying desperately to justify the boredom
As front door keys slash new coats of paint
Hoping to perpetuate the fallen empire
From the Pyrenees to the council estates
Voiced exploitation from the tribe
Everything must be destroyed N defaced

Support your local vandals
Support the aerosol kings
Support the white van pranksters
And the artists without funding

WEEKEND ROCKSTAR

Sixty hours a week on an agency sentence
Every outcome remains intermittent
Like a song that stays forever on repeat
A hundred miles per hour on a caffeine feed
Significant others acting as groupies
Cheering when the lines are cut
Living on a destructive tempo
And an appetite for the shops to never shut

Posing in the mirror with a stolen guitar
Signing damp beer mats at the side of the bar
A ride home in a stolen car chauffeured by your only fan
For the weekend rockstars nothing seems to happen

Five days a week you religiously behave yourself
Til the clock strikes Friday and you sacrifice your health
48 hours on the indestructible kick
Only to get back to detoxing in the routed week
Cheap wine and formaldehyde cigarettes
Consumed every fifty seconds
Waiting for the curtain call
That never seems to beckon

Posing in the mirror with a stolen guitar
Signing damp beer mats at the side of the bar
A ride home in a stolen car chauffeured by your only fan
For the weekend rockstars nothing seems to happen

DISTORTED SUNSET

Dust settles on sleepless tenements
Clouds form over wild grazers
Tissue bombs in chemical sleeves
Cosmic elements in cigarette papers
Where are the toxic criminals?
The sideways preachers
The gunpowder lecturers
The dynamite jesters
The devils in their blue dresses
The sirens with severed tongues
The children of everlasting innocence
That make my veins pump
Roman candles in furnished nests
Lecherous saints in weekend comas
The wired N frantic apostles
Desperate for life altering dramas

We look at one another
For stories to share
A fleeting glance
Gets us nowhere
We wait for the moment
For our chance to speak
We look at one another
With no connection to reach

Purge this soul of acceptance
Purchase this heavy heart
Gimme adoration N melodies
Under the distorted sunset

Distant sparks from furnished wombs
Let you know that the earth still breathes
It turns on the waste of a moment
And in the revolving minds that speak
Where are the controlled freaks?
The chaotic mercenaries
The villains, liars N perverts

That all the good girls seek
Vixens of gentle torture
Mothers of the strict agenda
Innocents of unexperienced sadness
Damsels of showroom fenders
Bleeding Romeo's on the corner of epiphany
Veterans of permanent inebriation
Battle hounds in the spaces of silence
Masters of continuous celebration

We talk but don't get close
We open up but never let in
That rhythmic eccentric pulse
That makes our lives spiral with a grin
We live for danger
Walking the same small world
We are strangers
Perpetuated by the same woe

Purge this soul of acceptance
Purchase this heavy heart
Gimme adoration N melodies
Under the distorted sunset

DJ

Morrisey was right
Hang the DJ
Hang him until we hear
The snap of his vertebrae
Let him choke
By his scrawny little neck
Let his setlist of popular bullshit
Suffocate him to his last breath
We heard that chart topper
Ten years ago
It was shit then
It's even worse now
As you pump your fist
And pose for the crowd
Channelling the Disco frenzy
Of European Trance
The banality of trendy hits
Making my ears bleed
We're not in Ibiza
We're in fucking Leeds
Another hardcore atmosphere tainter
Lost in the grooves
Thinking he's Pete Tong
While flicking through I Tunes
Confused by the intricate mechanism
Of fitting a needle to wax
Content to push buttons
On a technological etch a sketch pad
In fact I've changed my mind
Hangings too good
Instead we'll crucify him upside down
In the clubland neighbourhood
A public beheading
That'd do just nice
Shoot him with a lethal injection
So the monotony can be euthanized
Come the musical revolution
When we've disposed of Justin Beiber N Michael Buble

We'll start digging the graves
Of all the local DJ's

DANGEROUS MIND

Dark nights of the soul
Slaughter in a young girl's breath
Not like the other murderers
Everything different but still the same
Need a name to cry out
Need a threshold to drag you across
The world is a union of perverts
Lipstick cigarette smeared bloodstains
Can't differentiate
Intangible numbers in
Recycled business attire
Indifferent taste
Narrowed to conformity
In the peak hours

Murder N executions
Return the video tapes
Mergers N acquisitions
Nobody knows my name
Exhilarated
Satisfied
Obliterated
Dangerous mind

Outsider in the different time zone
Become the sadness of the target
Deep your feet in the civil butchery
In the abattoir of city heat
Stage hands commit suicide
Paint this life with bullet wounds
Fit the non-existing profile
A disadvantage of the heart
The earth swallows you up
Like the high water mark
On printed career paths
Dissolving in the trend
The money ball rolls
On the blood of stray cats

Mystifying N erratic
Impersonal shame
Homicidal N sadistic
Nobody knows my name
Exposed
Puerile
Disassociated
Dangerous mind

HARMONIC HEART

We share the same pain
Though we hide it well
I want something so badly
Only you have the answer to
The trees outgrow the rain
As your voice charges the bell
My snare drum heart beats madly
To your black N white blues

Ivory sensation ascends
We are so far apart
But the nerves of the soul deepen
By the sound of your Harmonic Heart

In ownership of the same weight
That drives us into the ground
We crawl to the fountain of youth
Only to find we've changed our minds
Our fates resting on an octave
Our songs light up the town
We're desperate for the whole truth
And never concerned of time

Ivory sensation ascends
We are so far apart
But the nerves of the soul deepen
By the sound of your Harmonic Heart

SURROUNDED

In amongst the dying leaves
In amongst the warehouse corridors that close in
Bombarded by driven snow
Enthused with the longing for control
There are men more poetic than I
Filled with humour N devoid of snobbery
There are more diligent and creative beacons
Uncorrupted by the stars
As I sit here N sulk
Trying to determine what is worthwhile
In amongst the revolving noise
In amongst the nervous insomnia
Tormented by the knowledge
That the universe is universal
In its overdramatic perversion
The brain merely a vessel
Overfilled with tainted water
There those who can write beautiful passages
Never for the world to read
And I hate them
And I love them all the same
For those linger in the air only to be consumed
When we're finally in the ground
I am surrounded by beauty I despise
By love that overwhelms me
In amongst the beer cans
In amongst the half smoked cigarettes
I sit and I wait
Through reason I cannot determine

COMPLAINTS

I've heard it all
I've seen it all
Just let me rest
Real rest
Like the uninterrupted sleep of a child
It's too hot in here
But if I turn the radiator off
The temperature will drop
And I'll end up back in the Antarctic
Of the damp tower block
I can't fucking win!
I think of rolling a cigarette
But that means I'll have to get up out of this chair
Which moulded into some impenetrable chrysalis
I don't want to write anymore
Can't somebody else do it?
I've been here
I've been there
I've seen it all
I've heard it all
When the fuck is the world going to disappear?

THE BLANK PAGE

There's been a poem lying around here for weeks
Shooting the breeze with the demon under my bed
They both chat shit about how I'm getting lazy
And the fact that I haven't unloaded the words in my head

The blank page wishes to be graphited
Like a whore that begs to be fucked
Wishing to be defiled N robbed of innocence
As I feel like a geriatric that can't get it up

It's been hiding in the cobwebs that I dare not wipe away
Lurking within the hinges of the door
Protruding in the wall where the damp stays
Skittering with abandon along the landmine floor

It nags like a partner I can never do right by
It appears like a friend from a forgotten past
It derails the unmaintained locomotive of thought
Leaving my mind filled with empty tracks

There's a short story in the notepad
That I need to devote myself to N construct
But my words are mere imitations
From the authors that had the ability to corrupt

There's limericks to be concocted
There's sonnets to compose
Yet the blank page stays as it is
Sooner or later I'll run out of odes

LIFE NEVER BEGINS

He's overdrawn on a payday loan
He's got a landlord that wants him out of his home
He's got a girlfriend he doesn't know
In a tight knit group where he doesn't belong

In the quiet of the tower block ballad
He's got money making tricks that always fizzle out
So he gets dizzy in his mate's bedsit
Another cheap high to smother the shouts

He's got favours nailed to the bone
He's got debts no man should own
He's got friends that leave well enough alone
With mounting messages on switch off phone

One day he knows he'll get it right
As he hustles in the bus station looking for a ride
Out for a job that he'll never keep
Because he wants for nothing in a life that never begins

THE MOMENT

The moment brings forth elements of unknown gateways
Senses damaged by the overdrive of internal significance
I walk past unopened doors in the undiscovered canyon
Waiting for the unrealised epiphanies that consume endurance
Deranged in the libraries of newly discovered processes
I lie awake at night with the mystery train in full force
Enthralled by the vivid mishaps of the human condition
Roads ready for development in the theatre of happenstance

The melody of the heartbeat still resonating
The orchestra of the circuitry still sounding brightly
The palpitation of the strands reigning tightly
The moment is an oasis not condoned by authority

Guided by strange figments within the familiar space
Dangling on the stars that shimmer through closed eyes
The re-arranged order still strumming at my mind
The formula holding me like an unmentioned stain
Picking the fleas off of the stallion's back
Reserved in the anger to emphasise the attack
No virtue afforded ins seizing the atoms that lost in the fibres of
evolution

The melody of the heartbeat still resonating
The orchestra of the circuitry still sounding brightly
The palpitation of the strands reigning tightly
The moment is an oasis not condoned by authority

SET THE WORLD ALIGHT

Don't sign me up for the revolution
I've got my own war to fight
Endlessly searching for who I am
Through the subway nights
Don't fill my glass with cosmic debris
I've got my own lesson to learn
My own line to walk
My own endless days to burn

You call my number
But it falls on deaf ears
I'm just trying to
Fight through the tears

Set the road alight
I'm looking for myself
Set the road alight
In case I'm someone else

I'm radicalized to numbness
I've seen it all before
I operate on routinized configuration
On wasted opportunities I crawl
Don't keep me in mind for inclusion
I won't answer your call
My independence prioritised
Leave this poor boy alone

You call me name
But I won't respond
All that I am
Has been N gone

Set the road alight
I'm looking for myself
Set the road alight
In case I'm someone else

CHAIN OF RESENTMENT

We didn't sign up
We didn't volunteer
We didn't ask to be born
But now we're here
Grasping at uncertainty
Immersed in ambiguity
And overloaded
With perpetual fear
Stranded in the overpopulation of bedroom revolutionaries
Lustful entertainment of headless numbers marching in rotation

On
A
Chain
Of
Resentment

Never given a choice
Or presented with an option
Ruthlessly uniformed
To the length of our participation
Clawing for independency
Unrewarded by individuality
Clung to mortality
Guided by misappropriation
Knowing so much only to be robbed of emotional attachment
The strain of our existence threaded in the tapestry

Of
The
Tightening
Chain
Of
Resentment

MEMORIZE

People don't like me reading from the page
But I just don't have the time
To sit down N revise
Every single line
That falls out of my leaking head
Recycling statements overused and overspent

People don't like me reading from the page
But I don't have a photographic memory
With the couplets that I scoff
Muttered with dread
That they've already been read
By worthless academics
Who can recite Shakespeare and translate it into Latin
While photo framing their so called careers

I like to take long shits
I like staring at the clouds
I just got off a 12-hour shift
I spend my evenings getting lost in crowds
All the familiar distractions
Keep me occupied
That's why I write this shit down
So I don't have to memorize

People don't like me reading from the page
It doesn't fit the mode of the slam
But I'll never be taken seriously
So who gives a damn?
People don't like me reading from the page
They it's unprofessional
Cos they think every basket house
Is a headline slot at Long Division festival

I'm enthralled by the dust that settles
Along the covers of books, I haven't read
And the duties that'll plague me
Until I'm found dead

With my eyes glued to the ceiling
With my cock resting in my hand
With notes scribbled on toilet paper
For poems I had planned
People don't like me reading from the page
By my competitive edge has died
I just don't have the stamina
To sit down N memorize

WINNINGS

Lucky fucking me
I've won enough for another
Dash on the scratch
That might land me a fiver
Two quid up
From what I've spent
Desperate for the big fortune
That never ascends
I want the last pickings
Where the big winners lie
Scrape off my retirement
Before poverty strikes me down
One-pound fifty
And I'm back where I started
Wondering if I should buy another
To cure this downheartedness
Itching for a lifetime
Overcome with panic attacks
Wishing the next ticket will be the one
Before my possessions are scrapped
Lucky fucking me
One more turn N I'm broke
Trapped in the limbo of empty pockets
Waiting for the punchline of the joke
Moments gambled on double sided paper
Money that I owe can be paid up later
Lucky fucking me
I get another try
To spend my wage
On opportunities that have passed me by
Lucky fucking me
I'm hooked on the strain
Of the good ol' greed
That assures me brain
That I'll own the Badlands
From the flick of the copper
But these winnings
Never seem to offer

The great escape
The golden pass promised to me
From the distant possibility from here to nowhere
These frightful winnings leave me bare

TWENTY QUID IN CHANGE

Two's on a rolly
A grain of sugar
Then you owe
The cheeky bugger
Ask a question
It comes with a fee
If you need a favour
He ain't the one to see
A formal greeting
Just in passing
He's straight on you
About what he's missing
A polite gangster
Whose connections are strained
The world owes him everything
Twenty quid in change

A slick emery
Stuck in your letterbox
Just to reel you in
On the compensation
A fixed penalty
On a handshake
Boasts about his county lines
While bumming smokes on break
Income on his mind
Currency his only goal
Windows dark from the inside
With an income from the dole
Leaving little bags along the street
Hoping to snag an investor
To his little circle of
Fiends and car park teenagers
Cuts you a line
Then snorts it himself
Saying that costs a tenner
And he'll be back to collect
Shows up on your doorstep

Windswept by the rain
His hand open wide as he mumbles;
"Twenty quid in change!"

PRIVATE N CONFIDENTIAL

The takeaway menus
Keep building up
Filled with appetisers
I'll never eat
The debts
Keep on mounting
With payments
I'll never meet
A tenant's survey
I won't fill in
A handful of scratch cards
From which I'll never win
A catalogue filled
With items I won't purchase
Final reminders
That I won't notice
My doorway
Filled with bills
The cost of living
Gives me chills
Bombarded by envelopes
That I won't open
Like odd socks
That need re-grouping
Loan payments
That remain overdrawn
Court hearing threats
That I ignore
Letter after letter
From unknown names
With unseen faces
Stating their claim
Strictly personal
Delivered by hand
Complaints from neighbours
That I can't stand
Property investors
And letting agents

Looking for clients
More numbers to the arrangement
Specialising in struggles
Of any condition
Negative equity
And dirty dispositions
Can I help find
A safe place
For a novelty
That's only available through Christmas
Networks transformed
From unseen connections
Brightly coloured
Important information
A little postcard
Saying 'Wish You Were Here'?
An unanswered question
For a price too dear
Five-star insurance
From a puppet with a catchphrase
Supermarket pamphlets
That leave me dazed
Direct lines
To unwanted quotes
For things I don't need
Cos I travel on foot
My new update
For a TV licence
Features, benefits
And augmented pay-outs
Another statement
For investment potential
Lick, sealed N stamped
Just private N confidential

HATE FREE

You know it's gonna be one of those days
When you burp and you can taste your own lung
As stale tobacco and last night's booze
Continue to party on your gums
You know it's gonna be one of those days
When you notice you're on the last sheet of toilet paper
And the opening notes to the 'Sound of Silence'
Play in your head over and over
You know it's gonna be one of those days
When Mr. Beamer refuses to indicate
And due to an onslaught of 10 second rain
The bus shows up fashionably late

When the milks gone off
And you can't have a brew
The electrics tripped
And you find a cat turd in your shoe
You come home late
Suicidal over trivialities
I'm hoping for the night
I can go to bed relatively hate free

You know it's gonna be one of those days
When you physically threaten inanimate objects
That won't respond willingly
To your actions
You know it's gonna be one of those days
When a brain fart leads to amnesia
And you get lost in your own home
Trying to find the keys to release you
You know it's gonna be one of those days
When the filth has cornered off the street
Because some naked crackhead
Is threatening to jump from his balcony

When some bloke at the urinal
Keeps giving you the eye
And sentimental waterheads

Keep demanding to know why
The earth isn't round
And why love fades
A man can lose his mind
In-between these days
All is shrouded in confusion
It's too dark to see
If I wake up dead
Perchance I'll be relatively hate free

5-YEAR PLAN

I don't need a 5-year plan
24 hours puts me under pressure
I consider setting me watch forward an hour
Travelling too far into the future
My senses have been corrupted
By the heat of the moment
I'm hardwired to malfunction
But set to never reaching an end

I don't need a 5-year plan
For all I know I could be dead
Paralyzed from the waist down
Or smoking through a hole in me neck
I could be surrounded by illegitimate offspring
And unable to keep my remaining faculties
Hopefully all of my appliances
Will outlive their warranty

I don't need a 5-year plan
60 seconds leaves me indecisive
There's just too much improbability
In one lifetime
I'm on the 30th level
Of this sensory immersive opera
If you see me say hello
For I'm likely to disappear

I don't need a 5-year plan
I'm stuck in the ulterior moments
Trying to fathom the here from now
Threatened by the past, future N present
Dragged through the doors of age
It's best to remain uncertain
Because as far as I can tell
The future is unwritten

IN THE END YOU BECOME YOURSELF

I'm a cowboy without a hat
And there's nothing worse than that
Another gambler without a deck
A sailor that can't tie a sheepshank
A singer without vocal chords
A junky that can't score
A poet lost for words
Robbed of the aspect of a metaphor

I'm all these things
And nothing in-between
In the end you become yourself
Such is the irony of destiny

I'm the sheik of araby
The mental health rep for the barmy
The man without a name
Playing both sides against the other
I'm a legend in my own lunchtime
A millionaire without a dime
I'm a concrete jungle boy
A ghost rider in the sky

Compromises clash with intentions
Dreams collide with reality
One world becomes another
In the hindsight of humanity

I wanted to be the Dread Pirate Roberts
But I'm a wannabee on the shelf
For better or worse
In the end you become yourself

CHANCER

If I was topical
If I tapped into the psyche
Of the social masses
And the contactless zeitgeist
If I spoke to the updated
Who can't tear themselves away from their phones
Then I'd hit the mainstream
And be with the rest of the posers
Who've cornered the market
On stating the obvious
Who've politically corrected themselves
To reach a potential audience

But I don't wanna make it
Death is more suitable
More rewarding than admiration
More fulfilling
Then living in a gold fish bowl
Surrounded by a stranger's gaze
I'd rather be a chancer
Than a sell out with a plan

If I had an agenda
If I protested on N on
About this N that
How nothing is right and everything's wrong
If I voiced my opinion
On what was said on the news
I'd have my own BBC documentary in no time
And be a storm on You Tube
I don't subscribe to bullshit
I don't even vote
I guess that sounds shocking
Compared to my other prose

I'm parlayed by the angels
Safe in the shroud of
Perilous anonymity

As I walk the streets
And smile thankfully
That nobody knows who I am
I'd rather be a chancer
Than a sell out with a plan

SEIZE THE NIGHT

There's piss on the floor
And a shit in the urinal
As the twilight attendant
Stands N looks puzzled
His wage in the ashtray
Filled with buttons N ruebles
With shrapnel N copper
To cover the cost of his burial
The barmaids in a strop
Cos Mr. Bombastic's too enthusiastic
Drunk on the atmosphere
Dancing like a spastic
As the young remedials
Are given plastic glasses
In case tempers flare
From the elephants on acid
Flyers used for beermats
Of a band nobody gives a shit about
Walking on broken chalices
Cos the cleaners got the night off
Lines snorted off of cracked tiles
Hallucinogenics imbibed from H20
A brief cigarette on the pavement
And the bouncers ask you to go
"Don't make her laugh she's got a Tena lady on"
Spouted by someone you wish you didn't know
The karaoke mic handed out
When the night moves too slow

All the cocktails are spiked
With someone's spit
Cos they've run out of dry ice
And there's nowhere to sit
The landlord doesn't like it
When you get too lit
To seize the night
You've gotta wade through shit

Can't hear fuck all
Cos the speakers are too loud
Can't get served
Cos the staff are having nervous breakdowns
A game of pools free
But the cues have been misplaced
After last week's knob head
Got a clap round the face
Just another dive
Where the punters complain
But aren't welcome anywhere else
Cos they have a fear of change
North face glad rags
From the 2nd hand boutique
As the arty existentialists
Think they're unique
While the safe urine quaffers
Every day of the week
Pick apart the pop culture universe
Not knowing their arses from their beaks

All the cocktails are spiked
With someone's spit
Cos they've run out of dry ice
And there's nowhere to sit
The landlord doesn't like it
When you get too lit
To seize the night
You've gotta wade through shit

WHERE'S MY AMERICANA?

Tin can lunacy and industrial disease
Big bad N beautiful urgent appeals
In the dirty sink of the industrial scene
Of the tower block ordeal
The dead left on the pavement
In supermarket trolleys
Decomposing in Indian summers
Where no one seems to notice
Terraces filled with landmines
Used jonnies and dead mice
A carton of lard to seduce the inflated queen
That fits much too tight

I want sandy beaches
And scantily clad damsels
Rather than been threatened
By a duffle coat munter with a pram
I'm stuck in the village green
Sinking in the black stuff
A character in a Morrissey opera
Where the fuck is my Americana?

A cold kebab and unwanted offspring
And a warm can of beer
A taste of flue and a stab in the back
Make a nice weekend souvenir
With dodgy cunts amazed by fireworks
And pilsner in a can
Kicking the shit out of phone boxes
And smearing insults on white vans
Happy pills N dirty water
Just to balance out the pain
Some dirty buzz N toilet seat concoctions
Brining catharsis in the rain

In the maze of retail parks
In search of genuine offers
Distracted by cricket

And undecided weather
The grass greener on every side
Outside the off licence
You stop and wonder
Where the fuck is my Americana?

DEBASEMENT

Dirty words are a myth
Designed to keep you dumb
Triggering the sensitivity
Of politically correct doldrums
Who think linguistic depravity
Holds no intellectualism
Yet one should breach the peace
Just to ease the reverence
Of moral conjectures
Through vulgar expletives
When nowt else will serve
Desecration brings forth catharsis
I couldn't give two tugs
Of a dead dog's scrotum
Of your stifled vocabulary
As you censor the emotional
Outbursts of the unsatisfied
Whose speech can be notated in grawlixes
Inside the social temples
With indifferent pejoratives
I can't pontificate my expressions
With technical alternatives
Or verbalize in accordance
To your polite niceties
I can't succinctly deliberate
My internal dysfunctions
I'd rather see you molested
Than have my language come into question
I hope barbarians bludgeon you
And violate your corpse
The next time you decide to correct
My articulation of choice
To be less objectionable
Holds no acceptance
It only brings contempt
Intensifying distance
The dialect of army creole
Is the language of sainthood

And as for the execration of piety
I couldn't give a tinker's cuss
Profanity is evidently elementary
For fools should not be suffered
I must state unequivocally in sheer debasement: YIPPE KAY YAY
MOTHERFUDGER

PRAISE

Where would I be
Without the other acts
And their partners
Waiting to perform?
Where would I be
Without the comperes
And the one regular
And his dog?

Bless those who actually show up
And put money in the busker's cup
Cherish the hosts who through routine
Make these nights the best places to be

Where would I be
Without the other bands
And their disinterested groupies?
Where would I be
Without the baffled landlord who looks
Around N says "Quiet tonight innit?"

Support the local hosts
Who get the names on the list
The ones who sit back N listen
To the prima donna's N starving artists
Raise a glass to the organizers
Propose a toast to the men N women
That spotlight the local talent
And make these places interesting
Praise be to the jolly motivators
And the midnight hound dogs
Praise the fellow chancers
Who unconditionally support us
Bless the watering hole presenters
Open to the possibility of new sounds
And for those who stayed at home
Perhaps we'll see you next time around

ROMAN CANDLES

The train shuttles along
On the songs of the
Untameable daughter's N sons
Who belong to the fix
The unexplainable trick
In the realms of the open mind

Complete in the restless toes
Who knows if love
Will guide us through these blues
That we release from our tongues
Under spotlight sun
Waiting on a sign

Eyes N heart fixated
On connections celebrated among
The silent stars elevated
Killing time with their ambition
Claiming their position
Before reality leaves them blind

Strangers look at their hands
As the songbird lands to greet
The congregation with a plan
To boldly N naively overthrow
Whatever seems to blow us
Away from this glorious time

Empty glasses hold the flame
Of fiery glances not returned
By meagre carnal chase
We will not let our hearts be polluted
In the commonplace duties
We are roman candles burning for all time

NEVER BIN' SPACE TRUCKING

I've witnessed fires on Greek hillsides
But the silver machine never took me for a ride
I marched in claustrophobic excitement into the depths of the
pyramids
But extra-terrestrial contact has always been denied
I've seen blackholes form at the end of desolate streets
But I've never made the jump to lightspeed
Skull fucked by rainbow strobe spasms
While longing to hear the recitation of Vogon poetry

No close encounters
No abductions from Coneheads
Intent on invading
No silent running
Through the final frontier
I've never bin' space trucking

I witnessed the Starchild trapped in a continuous loop
While longing to tread the flight deck of the Starship Enterprise
I've levitated over slabs of uneven pavement
But I've never seen the spotlight beam split the deserted sky
I've flown on the navigation of the endless moments
Wasted on the ambition of becoming a Starfighter
With tenement brickwork shifting to the pulse of tampered
perception
The laboratory concoction forcing my humanity to glow brighter

I wanted dinner with The Jetsons
In the restaurant at the end of the universe
But I'm fixated on the carpet that crawls
And laughter blossoming from the absurd

No close encounters
No abductions from Coneheads
Intent on invading
No silent running
Through the final frontier
I've never bin' space trucking

UNTIL THE CANDLE BURNS OUT

The streets
A vacant system
Of loneliness
Reaching the depths
Of ones
Own unique wave
Beckoning to
The discordant impact
Of our souls
As the cycle continues

Until the bell rings
Until the poet has shed his skin
Until the piano man
Ends it all with a wink N a grin
Until the last kiss
Before we see each other again
Until the high surges downhill
And quiet flashbacks force our minds to spin

Ones dreams
Rest in the wave
Of the sky
Dancing on
The air
Of floating absolution
I have
No reason
To fly
My destination continues into the unknown

Until the tension liquidates
Until the lunacy separates
Until the solidified
Dumbness hurtles N exhilarates
Just go with the feeling
No need to shout
Let us breach the forbidden territories

Until the candle burns out

THE CHAOS REIGNS STILL

There's a lowt in the kitchen
Ranting on about his connections
With a hippy in the hallway
Spouting his objections
As the ex-con
Deliberates his favourite flavour of crisps
And the blue wild angel
Tabs another trip
We've got Bollywood psychedelia
And eastern European rhythm
Mass hysteria N muddled accents
As the sunrise keeps its distance
As the blue eyed feline
Meditates within the congregation
On a solo flight to the cosmos
Of her own personal sensation
Feeling like rollercoasters we shout on balconies
Trying to engage each other's high
Desperate to tap into the spectrum
Seeing patterns when we close our eyes

We dance on uncharted waters
We strut through ungoverned lands
Looking for the reflection of our lives
Groping in the dark for a guiding hand
Within the limits of ourselves
Accentuated within the guarded city
We taste the kiss of bad love
Until we can no longer feel
High off the disco bulb fever
Emanating like pinhole spirals
Into the new realm we dig deeper
Into spirituality of the idols as the chaos reigns still

The cities electric eye
Burning harmoniously
As the pristine virgin
Decides to go home early

Pulses of sludge immersed
In industrial doom
As the take-off tricksters
Catch vibes in empty rooms
Distributing cigarette smoke
Bitch slapping us into consciousness
With chemicals mixed
On the kitchen worktop
Back to the 24-7 church
Where the bachelor gets mouthy
With a sweet little thing
Who wants his throat as a trophy
Staring into the distance
Within territories uncharted
Fantasy distorted by the reality
That in the morning we'll be right back where we started

I've tiptoed along the plates
That separated me from you
Building bridges that inevitably burn
Like all precious things do
Strutting through the mist
Under the fever trees
Ineffectually intellectual
As the fuse of the night burns then recedes
Born with the disgust of dystopia
Zombified by inherited diseases
Separated by tongue but connected in the final
As the chaos reigns still

TIME WOUNDS ALL HEELS

The good N the bad
The dull N the drab
The lucky accidents
The moments of impasse
One step forward
Two steps back
Between the present N the past
One cold outlook N the other filled with fear
Trapped within the sun N moon
Time wounds all heels

The hidden rules
That everyone forgets
The restless N the desperate
Need to confess
One slip of the tongue
And you regret everything you've said
Saddled with a brain that never forgets
20/20 hindsight like a slideshow reel
Between simplicity N insanity
Time wounds all heels

The attrition of sin
The mistake of experience
The punishing lows
The perils of significance
Out of misdirection
Comes a nagging insistence
That guilt is a permanence
That never yields
Yet forever is temporary
Time wounds all heels

When social imprisonment
Of modern slavery
Receding enjoyment
And misguiding bravery
When the dime is dropped

And the shit hits the fan
A nice little juxtaposition
Of a sensitive decree
Uttered by those who ought to know better
Time wounds all heels

TWO-MINUTE WARNING

Get your shit together
You can't come back
Say your goodbyes
While you've still got the chance
120 seconds
Then you are gone
Last call for anything
Before you go home
Hurry yourself up
Strike a pose
May God strike you down
You were born to lose
Take in the sunshine
Breathe in the air
Smile for once
Without a care
No regrets
There's no time
You never had enough anyway
So what's the harm?
Respond to the alarm
The night is dawning
Stay prepared for the two-minute warning

Fail to the system
That screams red alert
Concentrate on the sensation
Before every door shuts
No second chance
End all your business
No need to fight
Just cancel all commitments
It's a brief encounter
Just like every endeavour
All you need to worry about
Is getting there
Get over the hump
Death is eazee at the end of the day

The only thing you need to think of
Is what awaits you next
Whether you're stranded
At the pearly gates
Or you are unfortunately reincarnated
As yourself
You could be carried on the wind
And suffer this bullshit again
No time for mourning
After the two minute warning

TONIGHT

Tonight
The dust of the city lands softly on angels suicides
Tonight
Sirens in the midnight air awake the autopilot narcolepsy
Tonight
The songs of the world are heard through pirate radio dials
Tonight
The electrified waltz of kindship will save me
Tonight
Windows of the mind demand to be closed
Tonight
All the unlocked doors will be fixed
Tonight
All things that are determined will rest
Tonight
All will dissolve in the talents of independency
Tonight
The tour of the madhouses begins
Tonight
The rooftops will amplify the screams of the doomed
Tonight
All indulgences of the psyche are free
Tonight
We will decorate our awaiting tombs
Tonight
Dead anger will be nullified by amber serums
Tonight
Outraged craziness will be quilled by escapism
Tonight
All love is requited on the boardwalks of forsight
Tonight
The overly expressionistic millennials will escape derision
Tonight
We shall cheerily board the magic bus
Tonight
Alleyway cue cards own insistence
Tonight
All reactions will be necessary

Tonight
The hang man will cue the wire
Tonight
You and I will choke the last gasp of life out of this town
We will illuminate the abandoned movie sets of youth
Hot blooded and let go of restriction
Tonight you and I shall epitomise love, beauty and truth

SHOUT IN THE STREET

I live on scratchings
Left by the overfed
Guided by the voices
Inside my head
Within the shadows
Of the spendthrifts ghost
Riding high
On an all time low
I rule the deadends
Like an uncrowned king
Split in two
By the original sin
A public nuisance
In sickened sleep
Just a martyr
Who suffers deep
The slime of sewers
Coming after me
As I'm dragged
Through the vulgarity
Hell bent on destruction
The habit of attention
Provided with suspicion
Devoted to the action
Deadlines fall sort
All revolutions are cliché
Brief visits remain permanent
Through the nauseastic day
Suppression of vice
At the euphoria gates
Head in hands
Within the numerous pages
Follow the path
Of the older man
In the business production
That awards abandonment
Hatred N insult
Is the way of life

Complex identities
In optic night

HEAVENS ON FIRE

The priest with their pills
The girl's N their thrills
They're all out to get you
And you know they will
Surrounded on the one-way street
Where the hatred lies still
Suspended in the heat
Waiting for the kill

Heavens on fire!
Can't you see the light shining down?
Angels in their blue jeans
Out to extinguish that immortal sound

At the side of the road
Where fortunes are told
By the mystics with their tricks
That warn you to go
She says she's had enough
And wants to go home
She longs for her garden of dreams
Where no man has roamed

Heavens on fire!
Can't you see the light shining down?
Angels in their blue jeans
Out to extinguish that immortal sound

FIERY MAIDEN

Mixolydian fragments
Stringed scales
On blood oath fingers
Sweeping modes
In hare-brained fuzz
The body's resonance lingers
Shimmering frame
Bruised by
Internal spectres
Rosewood bite
Of Lydian subtlety
And Ionian sensation
Longed to be touched
By hungered eyes
In double paned displays
Prepared for mistreatment
In common time outrage
To the suitors at play
Screams of unison
In bended emotion
Of blistering volume
Mahogany log
With maple top
Of cutthroat precision
Born to be blue
With shimmering complexion
Of glossy inferno
Well of sound
A persistent hum
Of womanly candour
Sensitive tone
With adolescent howl
An anarchist's agenda rests with my fiery maiden

DEATH IS WELCOME

Death is welcome to my poems
A little light reading
Like a gossip magazine
When the soul remains healthy
Death is welcome to my agony
He can take it
Along with all the pieces
That were picked from my soul
By everyone I encountered
The grim reaper and me
We understand each other
We'll have a drink
And talk things out
Try to make sense
Try to understand
This consuming irritation
Of love and eternity
Death is welcome to the bastards
The slaves of the nine to five
The dreamers on the hill
And all of mankind disabled
By their internal malfunctions
Death is welcome to this poem
This boorish
Long winded
Perilous ode
That seems to be going nowhere
Death is welcome
To the dregs in the beer cans along the floor
The half smoked cigarettes
The programs on the TV unwatched
That I leave on simply for the notion of company
Death is welcome to you
But most of all to me
Waiting behind the curtain of another bad day
Take me away

BURNOUT

Let the burnout scream
Let his voice travel along the estate
Through the graffitted ginnels
With the last round on the reserved bench
Let him kick his heels
Like a child refused a gift
In the public slaughter
Of decency and common sense
I know that pain
I feel it everytime I look in the mirror
But my lungs can't summon the outrahe
Been that my tongue has been swallowed by the air
Let the burnout shout
Like God in the street
Disgusted by the motivation
Of those who hide the agony well
Let it crash through open windows
Let it disturb the distracted
Let this mismanagement of anger
Speak for us all
Let that expression
Of the threatening breakdown
From one who has had enough
Speak for us all
For we are all automated
And tightly wound
Like a rope that is ready to snap
Like an inherent vice
Ready to fall apart

UNLOCK THE JAIL CELLS

Roll the film
Play the song
Tune the guitars
Set the scene
Position the spotlight
Round up the pretenders
Pay off the pythons
Let the guilty go free
Hire the stage
Purchase the rights
Sign the contract
Clock in
Scratch the page
Rip the canvas
Hit the lights
Cure the ailments
Begin the soundcheck
Wake the compere
Wing the moment
Manipulate the mixing desk
Light the muse
Strike the match
Open the doors
Unlock the jail cells

THE GRIM REPEATER

He came in the early dawn
With scythe in hand
Ready to collect me
And dump me in the south of Heaven
The bell ran sporadically
As the letter box flapped up and down
With the door nearly removed from its hinges
As I abruptly came around
At first I thought it was the neighbour
Immersed I some hateful binge
Or maybe the police
Investigating another noise complaint
As I rushed down the hallway
Still adorned in my birthday suit
As I unlocked the chain
And forced down the handle
"What the fuck is this?" I shouted
"It's nearly four in the morning!"
As a cloaked figure glowered down
And pointed his bony finger at me
"I have to come collect you" he declared
In a voice similar to Barry White's
As he let himself in
And began to repeatedly switch on N off the lights
"Is this some kind of joke?"
I asked drunk N exhausted
As he told me in a malicious whisper
That my time was finally up
I demanded explanations
Or at least a reason
To why I now was on the verge
Of becoming out of season
This was surely a practical joke
Perpetrated by my mates
As I necked the last dreg
And asked him his name
"Mot, Thanatos, Giltine, Yamos
Call me what you like

No use in pleading for mercy
For your arse is well N truly mine!"
I stood N lit a cigarette
Thinking surely, he was taking the piss
As he looked around in disbelief
And asked: "How can you live like this?"
"What's wrong with it?" I queried
"What's wrong it's a disgrace
It's worse than bleeding Dresden!"
He raged while shaking his head in disgust
"This aggression will not stand"
He declared while rising to his feet
And before I knew it
He started to religiously clean
Armed to the teeth
With a range of disinfectants
Pledge, feather dusters
As he marched around acting like Mr Muscle
No bargaining for my soul
With a round of chess
Or a game of twister
As he kept on muttering "Cleanliness is next to Godliness"
Apron N rubber gloves
As he mopped the tiled floor
Matched my socks
And descaled the bathtub
He changed the duvet
Covered in cigarette burns
WD40'd the rusted cutlery
As I sat back N watched in awe
Polishing the door handles
Vacuuming the ceiling
Ingesting all the cobwebs
While incessantly whistling
Following me round with an ashtray
As I smoked on a chain
As I raided the cupboards
And stood over the porcelain not bothered about my aim
De-greasing the sofa
Complaining how my bare feet leave prints

And how I leave a trail of destruction
Even when I stay in my seat
Felix Unger in a skeletal frame
Locked in a compulsive timewarp
As I took myself off to bed
Deciding to depart
When I came around
The cloaked figure was gone
As my house glistened
And stank like a hospital ward
At first I thought it was a dream
Until I noticed the letter
Which read: I'll be back for you soon
You filthy motherfucker
As I crumpled it up on the carpet
That felt like freshly cut grass
I'll be ready the next time
The Grim Repeater comes back

GREENY

I couldn't help the shape I was in
When lost in poet's corner
With the booze in full swing
With my attorney insisting
We get another round in
Before we made it to the Irish Centre

Recognisable faces along the wall
As I lined my guts with watered swill
With the Jukebox repeating tracks from The Fall
With theories spouted N numbers rolled
My attorney chewing the edge of the bar
With tipsy strut we began our adventure

We made the trek
Towards East End Park
From the pumping bowels
Of lower Briggate
It'd be a night we'd never forget
As we marched to see the Blues messiah

I was fucked when I got there
Immaculate N twisted
As we doubled up on cigarettes
And questionable whiskey
As a mad woman began berating my attorney
Cos he couldn't control his humungous feet

A birdseye view
From the side of the stage
With his ES-335 on an easy chair
With my mind crazed
And heart ablaze
Immersed in the Albatross beat

The winter air
Sucker punched me in the face
Two hours had vanished

To which I could not retrace
As we both decided to continue the chase
The need to steal away the night

Flagging down cars
To take us back into town
As I puked on the pavement
Its colour lucid brown
Bad vibes dragging me underground
By overindulgence of delight
Slipping through traffic lights
Stumbling along the path
My mind N body interlocked
By the dirty wrath
Slobbering gibberish N slurred epitaphs
As we arrived back in the city

As the last orders bell sounded
As we made it to the Packhorse
We were soon surrounded
Like in an episode of Batman N Robin
By a trio of scoundrels
Who left us without a penny

Biff, bang pow!
Zip, Giff, Bing!
Knocked to the ground
And kicked once again
We fought em off drunkenly
Only to find ourselves shadowboxing

My attorney in a wave of emotion
Chased em down the alleyway
In a fit of commotion
Consumed in a heat of rage
Only to return with his nose broken
And his jacket covered in blood

The situation beyond our control
My attorney sought for sustenance

At the all night Macdonald's
As we were barred by security vultures
Who threatened to call the cops
As in the taxi home the radio played 'Man of The World'

SPITTING VENOM

I am the bird shit in your hair
The dirt in your fingernails
The burning in your bad heart
In the monotony of strangeways
I am the drunk in the corner
The spirit guide behind bars
Another soldier of misfortune
With a heart strung to the stars

Oh how I wish I could remedy despair
With a trick of the tongue
But smiles crack on pins N needles
When the fool is spitting venom

I am the insomniacs epileptic stare
The clock ticking inside the walls
The fibres of the funeral uniform
The dense atmosphere that crawls
I am the attention span of blinkered momentum
Just another another vessel without a spark
I am the cogs of the mind circulating
Striding on the hotfoot with verbal dynamite

Oh how I wish I could remedy despair
With a trick of the tongue
But smiles crack on pins N needles
When the fool is spitting venom

LONG TALL WOMAN WITH A BIG MAC

10 til 6 in the morning
When all I wanna do is sleep
Instead I'm faced with something
That I cannot unsee
I could smell it
Before it hit the window
That sweaty face hugger
With the 5 o clock shadow
Her mind warped by cocktails
And infernal disco
She lifts up her skirt
And my good mood goes
As the wide boys cheer
And the bouncers guffaw
While all her mates giggle
And cheer her on
I've heard of feminism
But this is all too much
As I get a full view
Of that clunge
Those peach fuzz lips
Her camel toe staining the glass
I'll never forget the night
I met the long tall woman with the big mac

REDUNDANT

Slip slide overdrive
Never had the will to survive
Just counting to the doomsday beat
In the slums
With the bums
Born without thumbs
Mingling with the stillborn breed

Tin pan Armageddon
Hear the levee's breaking
At the sound of the chime
On the last drag
Forced smiles crack
Epiphany lightbulbs turn black
In the aftermath of ordinary crime

Concrete chic
Amplified freaks
Slipping into another's skin
Red eyed
High flying
Dirty vibes
Waiting for a brand new thing

No use in being clever
Hope is for the innocent
Can't be bothered
When every opportunity is redundant

The vixen bleeds
Between the sheets
Shaking apart the cardboard walls
Left with an itch
From the bicycle seat
Of the mouthy bitch
Who spends her time on all fours

Flip, flop fly

In the disco dive
With the zombified N conquered
Bodies in suitcases
No occupational status
Everyday on hiatus
Every possession borrowed

Blind haze
Full of rage
Sustained on a small slice of nothing
Can't cope
No hope
On the downward slope
Cos there's fuck all worth knowing

No use in being clever
Hope is for the innocent
Can't be bothered
When every opportunity is redundant

FIGMENT OF MY OWN IMAGINATION

My name is on the bullet
I'm recognized in broken glass
I appear on empty lists
I am a memory of the past
I'm there in the deleted scenes
Scrambling across the cutting floor
An apparition in suburban deserts
A draft waiting behind the door

I don't exist
I'm there and then I'm gone
I'm a figment of my own imagination
Hoping to belong

I'm lost within a strangers photo album
My voice is a whisper in the ground
In the industrial wasteland
A melody imbedded in silent sounds
Numbered N filed away
Nowhere but in-between
A man of smoky twilight
Longing to be seen

You hold my hand
To feel a cool breeze
You call my name
Waiting for a reply
But I'm drifting
On the rollercoaster tempo
That remains the same
As time moves on by

I don't exist
I'm here then I'm gone
I'm a figment of my own imagination
Hoping to belong.

CREEP METHOD WIRED STYLE

Porcelain smiles
Freakishly wild
Plastic handshakes
Creep method wired style

Hey up sunshine
How's your dad?
How's this N that?
What's yours is mine
Hey up stranger
How's work?
Keep your chin up
No danger
How you doing?
You hear about whats his face?
Fucking slipped the net
Won't see him again
Hey up bruv
How's your health?
You're looking well
Where's that money you said you'd cough up?
Eazee chum
Where's the love?
How's your luck?
Too fucking bad
Every where's tough
I'll see you around
Just remember
To keep it slender
And everything'll be sound
Keep your mouth shut
Keep your dreams to yourself
Keep your dick in your trousers
And worry about your mental health
Do as you're assigned
Deafen your interest
Close your mind
Just like the rest

It was good seeing you
See ya mate
Stay safe
And remember what I told you

Stay unedumucated
Stay unorganisized
Keep busy
Creep method wired style

IT KILLS TO BE ALIVE

The doctor knows what you have
Cos he's got it too
Directed by pamphlets on dementia
And the best way to go to the loo
Take this prescription
It could very well help
If not then you're better off
Consulting someone else

Plenty of rest N you'll be fine
But don't forget you gotta be up at five
Every morning right on time
To fit the profile you didn't design

Strung out
Shagged
Red eyes
Bad back
Wellbeing week?
Don't make me laugh
These days
It kills to be alive

Change your diet to an energy drink
To be consumed fifty times a day
Here's some placebos
To white wash the pain
Rainbow coloured uppers
Immersed in side effects
Multi coloured downers
That leave your soul for rent

No excitement and you'll be right as rain
No hurt/ no power/ no discomfort/ no gain
Keep the cylinders burning until you reach your grave
Or until you spontaneously combust on a pharmacy opiate

Burnt out

Frazzled
Weak nerves
Bad heart
Wellbeing week?
Don't make me fucking laugh
These days
It kills to be alive

RED SEA

I was facing redundancy
So they changed my shift
From the solitude of nights
I was back in the market
Of hairbrained shoppers
Thriftless consumers
Big spenders of boredom
All tallying up the sales targets
People are scum
One on one they are not so bad
But in the heat of purchase
You can spot the evil in everyone
You can see the desperation
Within the blink of an eye
As they recede in trauma
When the special offers passed them by
They just can't take it
It's as if their entire being
Their entire existence
Rested on this moment
As the bins pile up with receipts
Stock is dropped in the wrong place
One born every minute
As you are surrounded by blurred faces
Soon enough she walks in
Thick green parka in summer heat
The smell of piss
As she mumbles to herself
Shopping trolley dragging behind her
As she makes her way to the toiletries
Props herself against the shelf
And shoves her hand between her legs
Ruffling under her duffle skirt
She places the soiled handkerchief
The bloodied feminine towel
In an empty box
That has forfeited the need to be recycled
As she thumbs through the range

Of multi coloured disposable protection
Rips open the packaging
And without hesitation
Replenishes her necessity
And walks out the door
As I adjourn for a cigarette
I've said it before
And I'll say it again
People are scum
And that's the end

IT AIN'T ME

You want me conscientious N practical
A smiling face devoid of a conscience
Loyal N gullible
Not a trace of independence
You want me ashamed N desperate
Bereft of any ideals
You want me disposable N disenfranchised
If I had any hope you'd steal it
You want me desperately suicidal
I can see you waiting for the levee to break
I can't be excepting N laidback
Playing this loaded game
You want me braindead N austeritized
A happy little representative
Invisible N dehumanised
Another zero-hour fugitive

I'm not what you want
And I never will be
I'm not what you want
It ain't me

You want me to nod in agreement
To everything you say
You want me to jump to every notion
That slivers into your out of date brain
You want me to pay attention
But I'm too fucking angry
Too fucking stupid
And too fucking dull N dreary
You want me to be enthusiastic
Dumb N domesticated
To keep me cautious N keep me scared
Another lamb to euthanasia
Every though that crawls into your head
Is a bad idea gone wrong
I'm on the losing end once again
To whatever the fuck you want

I'm not what you want
And I never will be
I'm not what you want
It ain't me

So you can take your
Finely tuned
Strictly groomed
Fascist motives
And your
Two fisted
Double standard
Conformist agenda
And all your misinformation
And all your cruel intentions
Your sick
Deluded
Confounded
Petty minded bullshit
That makes me wake up in the middle of the night in a cold sweat
Your garish rewards
That are supposed to make me swoon
When all I wanna do
Is vomit on your nice
And laugh
In your no vacancy face
So take your cheap
Wasteful existence
Your viscous
Perverted malice
And kindly
Do yourself in

I'm not what you want
And I never will be
I'm not what you want
It ain't me

NOTHING EVER WORKS

Can't get a connection on my feed
Need a smoke but I got no money
Need a hit but my dealer can't be seen
Need work but my hours were cut
Need a drink but the shop is shut
Can't move cos everything hurts
In the end nothing works

Need a fix to bring me round
Had a cat but it drowned
Had a girl but she left town
Need religion without the church
Can't afford to fill my cup
Everything ends and that's enough
In the end nothing works

Need you but you're not here
Social company costs too dear
Need a high without the fear
Direct debits leave me stuck
Taken for a ride by shiftless crooks
In the crossfire where uncertainty lurks
In The end nothing works

MILENNIALS

Tobacco sunrise over abandoned cardboard lodgings
Windows burn like matches in the screensaver landscape
Eternal sanctuary on vacated gold courses
All signs lead to the exit that holds no escape
We're never gonna make it
But we're happy to be lead
Along the backroads of promises
That we never truly believe
We strive for the higher ground
To which we'll never reach
The incentive of our ideals
Never matches our thrifted currency
Backwards is our direction
The road to nowhere is our home
On the dark road of no authorisation
Flickering like flies around a dimming bulb
Lumbered with the mistakes
Of someone else's fantasy
Marooned in the uncertainty
That heaven was cleared out yesterday
In the tunnel of mirrored ceilings
Music flowing through wallpaper leaves
Light draws ever near
As whispers are heard within the unknowing
Here we are
Nowhere in particular
Watching
As the sun goes down
Change of heart
Renegades of routine
Searching
For the unheard sound
Longing
For amphetamine epiphanies
Lovelorn
Damaged
Ready to traipse
Through the dark roads

In search of eternity
Now we're here
Deciding the next move
Determining
Which direction the wind blows
Crossed minds
Tangled hearts
Of impetuousness
Restless hysteria grows
Looking
For the mardi gras
Locked
In indecisive guts
The chance of anything
Holds the same outcome

NO DESIRE FOR ME

Let me read through your private footnotes
Let me tip toe in secret through your roads
Let me snicker by in lieu of your contact
Let's pretend this is the first time we've ever met
Let me be present to your wayward follies
Let me rule the backgrounds of your unprocessed cosmic movie
I wanna see where the line is drawn
I wanna cross the threshold to which the bough breaks

Listen to my heart
Listen to its crooked beat
It shuttles like a freight train
Of softened wind
It's sound but a murmur
Like a flattened bass drum
Listen to the vibe
Of the nerves that sing

Let the drums beat out of time
Let the song be slightly off key
Play the guitar and leave it untuned
The strings of the piano have no desire for me

Let's look to the future that is already over
Its rewards offering nothing but none
Let's think of the fortune that's already been spent
Our repentance is premature in the moment that's gone
Let me take your chemical potions in the midst of the depraved
Let me listen to the lesson of those who'll never fade
Let me take the last scrap of your conscience
And leave you crying in the banishing rain
Let me feel the comfortability in your shoes
Let me convince you that your hopes are lost
Let me give you a ride to the abandoned haven
Natural highs ready to diminish you at any cost

Listen to my heart
Listen to its crooked beat

It shuttles like a freight train
Of softened wind
It's sound but a murmur
Like a flattened bass drum
Listen to the vibe
Of the nerves that sing
Hear my disobedience
Listen to its futile cry
It blazes in the haze of opposition
When my wounds are pricked
Let me fool you
Mishear my uncontrolled sadness
As I take my position
In the uncalculated mood swing

Let the drums beat out of time
Let the song be slightly off key
Play the guitar and leave it untuned
The strings of the piano have no desire for me

BE YOUR MAN

Cool N calculated
Like a con with a trick
Distantly close
With your presence to let

You look different
But you are the same
You speak sideways
And your mood is strange
I can't read you
Nobody can
Nothing to do
But be your man

You are by my side
Which is a lightyear away
Like my mind
That doesn't wanna stay

You look different
But you are the same
You speak sideways
And your mood is strange
I can't read you
Nobody can
Nothing to do
But be your man

RATIONED SPECTACLE

If I could go back
I surely would
Back to the point
My blood was spilt
My hand a cup
Emptied of its contents
If I could sing
I'd raise my voice
In the congregation
Of athletic noise
I've had enough
Of critics consent

Waiting on a miracle
Distracted by the sign
That what is yours is mine
In the rationed spectacle

If I could turn the clocks
I'd pay the fine
To repeat the scene
Where your eyes left mine
A thought on my mind
Repeated like an advert
When I turn around
Will I find you waiting?
Or would you leave town
Because I'm beyond saving
Just proof I'm not the kind
Whose life is not worth the thought

Waiting on a miracle
Distracted by the sign
That what is yours is mine
In the rationed spectacle

If I knew the place
Where all things changed

I'd take a trip
To see the remains
Of what is left
Of our unbreakable vow
I've had enough
Of this suffocating guilt
That maroons me in the Badlands
Where affections are refused
If this is death
Then let it be anyhow

Waiting on a miracle
Distracted by the sign
That what is yours is mine
In the rationed spectacle

HANGING TREE

I fought in your corner
All the while the funeral mourners
Insisted I take my own life
I practiced at the crossroads
For forty nights or more
So I could sit comfortably in the spotlight
Wasting away in the shade
Burning in the deep freeze
I've nothing left to say
So leave me here to please
My sordid impressions
I'm dangerously close
To reaching the hanging tree
Where all the kindly souls
Left their ropes for me
In hopeful discretion
I declared war on content
When all my youth was spent
In the corridors of waiting
In the realization if the message
Misheard and misrepresented
In the interpretive sin
Dust in the breeze
Atomised by your sighs
Your tongue as fierce
As your breath that drives
The throws of my attention
I'm dangerously close
To the hanging tree
Where all the kindly souls
Left their ropes for me

BREAK THE VOW

Take all your drugs
And empty menus
These bare bones
Remain unstained
Take all your songs
And chicken scratch platitudes
The meaning always
Stays the same
I won't follow
On your crusade
I'm not an apostle
To your lurid games

Not no way not no how
It's time to break this vow

Abandon all hope
Like a sinking ship
Soon enough these days
Will leave you sick
I'll give you back
Those remarks of wit
And refill the bottle
That made you lose your grip
We don't need you
Never did, never will
You're just another fool
On the sermons hill

Not no way not no how
It's time to break this vow

NO REMORSE

Spit into the open mouths
Of the invisible choir
That sing your ballad
In your final hour
Relight the dimming
Candle at your bedside
Before your last breath
Ignites like a disappointed sigh

Flip the bird
To the one N only
No remorse
Just eradicated sentimentality

Scratch away the headlines
Of the invitation
Delivered to your door
By the angels of anticipation
Scriptures full of cigarette burns
Psalms used as toilet paper
Here we are waiting
For the point where we'll never remember

Flip the bird
To the one N only
No remorse
Just eradicated sentimentality

WINDLESS CALM

I hear the violins
With mathematical urgency
The soundtrack of my life
Beating fast
I look over my shoulder
And I see nothing
But at times like these
The way things are never last
The stench of death
Waits for me on the corner
Like a sugar plumb fairy
With a bag of delights
Like an electric eye
Watching my every move
I tread carefully
Through the streets that bite

I wanna go crazy
I wanna cause harm
I want my heart to have some hunger
But I'm lost in the windless calm

The orchestra of shame
Performs languorously
Inside the highways
Of my rearranged brain
The beating drum
Of time catching up
Crawling over the broken glass
From nights of the insane
The poisonous rhythm
Invading my ears
As I'm trailed
By the lost years
There's no going back
Just move ahead
Along the road onward
Like the tracks of tears

I wanna go crazy
I wanna cause harm
I want my heart to have some hunger
But I'm lost in the windless calm

LOST IN THE OCEAN

I'm never drunk enough
I'm never high enough
These intoxicants are premature
I'm too tired
I'm too wired
To worry about expenditure
The circuits don't fit
The mainframe doesn't compute
I'm lost in the aftermath
Of someone else's blues

I refuse the mainland
The desert was flooded long ago
Lost in the ocean
Overrun with filth and lotharios

I never sleep
Long enough to keep
The impression of the dream
I guess I'm fucked
Shit out of luck
Like all the wasted youth before me
Broken pieces can't be pieced together
When pulled apart by neglect
Every where's a one way street
Filled with the stench of regret

I refuse the mainland
The desert was flooded long ago
Lost in the ocean
Drowning in the filth of ego

BANISHMENT

You'll get caught
Sooner or later
Soon enough they'll realize
You're not worth the time
All of your information
Shown to the blind
They'll catch you unaware
When your pants are down
And organize a parade
When you leave town
They know
You owe
The ferryman
But you
Spend your life
In banishment
You'll be bought
And accused as a traitor
In the clarity of eyes
That witness your crimes
The walls painted in your frustration
Witnessed by distracted minds
Surrounded on the stairs
Without a sound
Living without a care
In the unending streets underground
They know
You owe
The ferryman
But you
Spend your life
In banishment

MIRACLE

We were never meant
To walk the line
Our shine wore off
Over time
Innocence
Is just a passing phase
We re but angels
With no saving grace

Holy mechanised
Spiritually unsatisfied
Lost in the genocide
Of a purpose unclassified
Silent witness
To the indefinable miracle

We were never meant
To blindly worship
Money hungry
Purveyors of tricks
Made up of the patterns
From the stitch of mistake
Consumed in the fabrics
Of chance too late

Holy mechanised
Spiritually unsatisfied
Lost in the genocide
Of a purpose unclassified
Silent witness
To the indefinable miracle

THIS HOLE OF MINE

Lay your hands upon me
Feel my aching bones
Tell me I'm the only
When you want to be alone
Seek me in the wasteland
Find me in the crosshairs
State your destination
I will meet you there

Let me feel your cold embrace
So you can check my pulse
Let me watch you silently
Until I've had my fun
My soul lurks in open doorways
My heart waits in confessional booths
My mind an overfilled glass
Containing second hand truth

Make me a believer
Tattoo your facts
Along my curious mindscape
Let the mile in your shoes
Burn within my soles
Like a notion that irritates
I'm at your disposal
A guiding light of mesmerising crime
Look down upon me
As I dig this hole of mine

DEFAULT SETTINGS

Moving to the rhythm
To the tune of the city
That's notated in single file
Minor key voices
Pontificating their obsessions
In undertoned needful sighs
The music in their veins
Anesthetized to a low hum
That's cemented to 4/4 time
As they remain on auto pilot
From Xanadu to the slums
Prosecuted for their social crimes

I don't wanna talk
I don't wanna know you
Just make sure you stay outta my way
I'm not your friend
But I can fake a smile
These default settings help me through the day

Consciously in contact
With the wavering emotions
Set to commit me to insanities grasp
Blinded by the certainty
Consumed by social conformity
And the nagging ghosts of the past
Hardwired to social repulsion
Deeply and literally self-centred
Adjusted to the daily exercise
The imperial pettiness
Of the servant and master
Will one day beg for each other's suicide

BENCHRATS

I can hear em
When the lights are low
As they sing world cup songs
Outside my open window
That I can't close
Cos it's too damn hot
Sweating my balls off
In my half empty cot
Laughing and jeering
Drunkenly insisting
That it's coming home
As I pray during the next match the ball explodes
Desperate to go to sleep
Because I have to be up at six
To get to a job
That makes me feel sick
I'd be getting pissed too
But I'm needed on the shop floor
At stupid O' clock
Wondering what my life is for
One needs a light
For their badly rolled spliff
As one accuses the other
Of putting words in front of everything
Illegal humans
Looking for a good time
Barred from the chains
And the noisy dives
I am a Golden God!
One of them proclaims
No you're just a piece of shit
That's keeping me awake
As they carry on
Until the dawn
I wish they'd all fuck off
And leave me alone
The sound of broken glass
Echoing from the pavement

As I toss N turn
From the cheers of derangement
Hanging round when the world stops
Bottled dreams in shopping bags
Eyes pinned back in search of the cops
As I spend the night with the benchrats

ANGEL IN DISGUISE

She's out to kill
She's out for blood
Heads will roll
Don't play the hero it'll d no good
The fucker will rue the day
The guilty will be prosecuted
She'll make you wish
You were neve conceived
Just hope to die quickly
If you get in her way
Don't count yourself lucky
Because mercy holds no sway

She's fierce
Unruled N savage
She is the prize
Dangerous
Incorruptible
An angel in disguise

She won't budge
Not for anything or anyone
She's refused the Garden of Eden
And killed the seventh son
She's played the devil
And fooled the angels
Nobody has a chance
When she turns the tables
When she makes her stand
Against the world that turns
Her voice a battle cry
That resonates through the years

She won't be bought
She won't be sold
She won't toe the line
She's deadly
With lightning tongue

An angel in disguise

PRACTICING WITH LIFE

I'm not sure
I can't be certain
I can't commit
I won't determine
How the morning will begin
How my day will end
I'm just moving slowly
Around the cosmic bend
I can't commit
There's too much at stake
I will never be
What you want me to fake
Time is for the taking
Moments are for wasting
No point in chasing
The memories that keep fading
To savour anything
Is simply pointless
Sins are but bruises on the skin
To which we refuse to confess
I won't play ball
I'm not for trade
I won't keep the goal
I refuse the parade
I can't tell
I don't know
Modern livings
Made my brain slow
I refuse the obligation
No more contracts to sign
From this day on
I'm practicing with life

TIM

The future is bleak
For someone like Tim
Living on the streets
His chances are slim
Ever since his dad
Kicked him out
Declaring
"There'll be no fuck ups in this house!"
He's sick to the back teeth of the late nights
His son coming home drunk and pissing in the oven
The police knocking on his door at all hours of the morning
And on top of all that he's knocked up his first cousin
For not holding down a job
For not leaving his bedroom
For picking his toe nails in the lounge
And using his credit cards to download porn
Now Tim's life
Is filled with desperation
The only shelter from the cold
Is in the all night bus station
Eating out of bins
Living in doorways
Trading sexual favours
For a place to stay
With your generosity
You can help put an end to this
To make sure that someone like Tim
Can get his benefits
For two pounds a month
With your help and support
You are helping to make sure
Someone like Tim is rescued N rehomed
We will send you weekly updates
Of Tim getting his fix
On baccy, takeaways
And Holbeck business
Tim can't ask you for help
But we can

Go to adoptawanker.co.uk
And save a life now

A BAD IDEA GONE WRONG

The live fast icon
Hoping to be a good looking corpse
Sold his soul for profit
And an unstable horse
Who eats up the income
Like rotten apples
She's too pissed to function
And too hot to handle
He had a dangerous edge
And a voice with bark
 Lust for life N need for speed
Before headhunted by the panel shark
Got a deal
On lightweight records
Toned down his language
Keeps the hits placid eating cucumber sandwiches
Dotted signature
On the straight line
Two years in the studio
To discover nobody's got the time

Another has been
A used to be
A could've been
A music awards accessory
A sell out
A money grubbing parasite
A bad idea gone wrong
Deserves no 2nd thought

Started on the folk nights
Hoping to get rich quick
Platinum bankcards
And cheerleaders bouncing off his dick
Lumbered with stale beer
Rather than caviar and champagne
No limo escort
So it's the bus home in the rain

Filled out the entry form
To stop been a stockroom assistant
Hoping to get on TV
With the rest of the attention seekers
A talent show bell end
Waving the flag of patriotism
Gets to the final round
To become the main judges new gimp
Forgot about the music
Traded his guitar for a backing track
Now he's on the pantomime circuit
Wishing he could go back

Another has been
A used to be
A could've been
A music awards accessory
A sell out
A money grubbing parasite
A bad idea gone wrong
Deserves no 2nd thought

POETRY BLUES

Help I need assistance
His pen doesn't match my heart
My guts are ceasing up
Soon I'll be afraid to fart

Help I'm getting pretentious
My words are turning soft
I fear if I write another line
The angel of death will kill himself off

I'm as giddy as a suedehead
Loitering at the side of a grave
I've got the poetry blues
Fragile is my middle name

My fronts beginning to rust
I'm as excited as a self-harmer
Whose got an electrical socket by the bath
Having been subjected to mild drama

Help I've contracted ennui
And I fear it might be terminal
One more resentment to purge
And I'll be planning my own funeral

I'm researching political conspiracies N knife crimes
So I can appear topical
It comes from having a lack of talent
And the eternal internal struggle

I should have taken some advice
And stuck to manual labour
Knuckled down until my retirement
Rather than documenting every failure
If you write while you are depressed
Then don't take it up as a living
There are better career options
Hell, what about advertising?

Help I need a paramedic
At least a doctor with a clue
I'm tired of this delicacy
This overly sensitive hue
I'll stick to writing limericks
And fuck off these poetry blues

YOU ONLY DIE ONCE

Find your madness
Hone your insanity
I impeach you
To nurture the craziness
Of your straight jacket fashion
Brave the sadness
Inherited in humanity
I beg you
For I shall wear the scars
That sought to plague N leave me damaged

Don't be curtailed
Or brainwashed
By someone elses insistence
Let your freak flag fly
For everyone to see
Cos you only die once

Discover your eccentric
Dispopularity of the norm
For you will find
Infinite worlds upon worlds
Ready to be invaded
Let that absurdity shine
Through every storm
And don't pay any mind
To the thieves N the squanderers
Of the great gift we cannot save

Be determined
In your commitment
To the lone N the lost
Don't be mistreated
By a stranger's exploitation
For you only die once

BELL ISLE KYLE

I'm a ghetto disciple
I work the night shift
20 hours a week
Stacking shelves
I've got more unwanted offspring
Than a German beer market
The Jeremy Kyle show knows me
Very well indeed
Two up two down
With me mother and her cat
I have to be home on time
Or the cheeky cow locks me out
I told her that I'm a grown man
And that I can do what I want
But she said "A grown man wouldn't
Wear his cap indoors N sleep with his bedroom light on"

I'm an estate idol
I run these streets
I've had more orgies
Than hot dinners
I've been shot, stabbed, drawn N quartered
All the coppers know me shoe size
I'm known as Escobar to the catnip addicts
And prince charming to all the mingers
I've got shares in Ladbrokes
And unused phone boxes
My pockets
Are currency fireproof
I'll do your online shopping
For you
Then finger your sister
Up the duff

I'm Bell Isle Kyle
I'm known all over town
Connected with the Armley menthols
And the LS14 Clowns

A suburban gangsta
The apple of me mothers eye
But don't tell her what I get up to
Cos I'll be grounded for the rest of me life

I'm a playground outlaw
And I'm notorious
Carbonated smile
And green fingertips
I'm due in court til the end of the month
For not meeting me repayments
Due to the bitch who said she was fixed
While smoking all of my cigarettes

I'm Bell Isle Kyle
I may be middle aged
But I'll do anything on a dare
Just another bedroom MC
Living life without a care
I spit rhymes about my connections
And how my life is so terrible unfair

SCHOOL NIGHT

All the weekend warriors are sleeping
Alarms set for the next working day
The white horse closes due to a power cut
As the righteous party goers raid the takeaways

She should be at home
Cosy in bed
Secure in an elaborate dream
As the man in the overcoat
Lights a cigarette
And waits to get his money
Dirty deeds for a pocketful o' nowt
Everyone plays it safe on a school night

She's fourteen speeding into middle age
As she struts the fractured streets
As the tuxedo pimp grabs her by the elbow
And spits "Where the fuck have you been?"

I mind my own
And continue home
In need of another beer or two
As she hands over the cash
And he slaps her arse
Saying she should change her attitude
Grisly business
Until harsh morning light
Everybody plays it safe
On a school night

DON'T MIND DYING

I saw the queen with the black N white heart offer up her secrets to a
half empty room
As her hangers on waited for their money
I saw the Buddhist with his dancing stick squawk like a chicken as
the rhythm of the
Tape deck captured the groove in his blood
I saw the Quarry Hill protestors sing a song about a doorway saint
lost in the front page
Of headlines from yesterday
I came to see you tonight unable to remember the reason for my
existence as the epileptic
Lights flicker having waded through shit N mud

The tracks of our years
Flowing from the speakers
In the hairbrained night
Time runs away
From the grasping hands of the day
I don't wanna leave this life, but I don't mind dying

I stood in awe as the music man ravaged every available instrument
inside of the acoustic
Monastery
Dancing, chain smoking, chatting shit N hoping that I could be stuck
in these moments for
The length of my waning thread
I raised a toast N pondered over heavens realism as the pin dropped
and the hammer met the
Anvil
Praying that this glorious, righteous beauty in which we linger was
the reward for my
Unrealized death

And when the last note rings out
In the fortress of the open mind
I'll be there
Trapped within the ovation
Awaiting the crescendo

Of this imperfect cadence

The songs of youth
Given as proof
That we once thrived
The tracks of our years
Flowing from the speakers
I don't wanna leave this life, but I don't mind dying

CUNTRY LIFE

Trade your safety pin armour
For a tweed jacket
Comb your hair
And learn to be polite
Swap your guitar
For a hunting rifle
Marry an existentialist solicitor
Safe in a trust fund
Swap sex for dinner parties
Spit N vomit replaced with cocktails
Anarchy is staying up past your curfew
And not checking your emails

Think about your public image
Seen by the rest of the plebs in the village
You'll soften over time
Settle down N get used to your Cuntry Life

A tuxedo in place of leather
Statements replaced by name brands
Hate soon turns to complacency
Ideology corrupted by finance
Ideals are meant for the young
Sober up by the thought of survival
You failed at your rage against resentment
Now your goal is to remain idle

Herbal tea rather than the adhesive buzz
Sedation through afternoon soaps
The state of the weather is your only gripe
Calm yourself down and get used to your Cuntry Life

Three chords exchanged for eazee listening
Rage deteriorates into servitude
The backbeat slows to a murmuring pulse
You never got anywhere being rude
You never had a chance anyway
Rebellion never seems to last

You're just another entry in trivial pursuit
Now sit in front of the camera N recall your past

Gathering moss N fading away
Sooner or later you won't even remember your name
It's either this or the 9 to 5
I hope you're sitting comfortably in your rotten Cuntry Life

A LIFETIME IS NEVER ENOUGH

I fear I'll never see
Sharknado 18
Or Jeremy Kyle reappear on TV
Or the Beatles Black album to be officially released
I'm afraid I won't be around
When dubstep is abolished
Or when Simon Cowell's put in the ground
And the council start work on something they can actually finish

For The Smiths to get back on tour
And Michael McIntyre to give up
I won't get to witness these things
Cos a lifetimes never enough

I know I won't see the Sisteen chapel
Cos me pockets are always empty
And as for moving to Mars
You're best waiting another century
I fear I won't see
Found footage of the Golden Girls having an orgy
But there's no point in been downhearted
Cos existence holds no expectancy

So little time
With too much to do
These hopes are in the pipe with other dreams
Cos a lifetime is never enough

KEEP PORN ON THE INTERNET

If they bang porn off the internet
They'll start fucking in the streets
They'll save themselves for the park bench
Rather than in-between the sheets
Fitting glory holes
Into every city centre cubicle
Drilling into every wall
So they can get their fill
All those sodomy starlets
Not fit for prime time TV
Not big enough for soap operas
Watched by your granny
Will start gargling hugs in public
For a nominal fee
That little cumdumster
Won't have a pot to piss in
As soon as she loses the subscribers
Who long for her to stay in the missionary position
If they bang porn off the internet
They'll arrange public showcases
Deep throat in the playground
And the Living Statue Takes It in The Face
In the Maccy D's drive thru
Like the cure for aids has been discovered
It's just another gig
For those desperate for attention
Live broadcasts on the feednets
Notifications on social networks
Dogging becomes a career statement
On a CV intended for the role of office clerk
Those 'step siblings'
Who can't control their urges
Will be caught dry humping
At next Sundays church service
Swingers will start trading
In the local market
And all those secret cottagers
Will get their own reality TV series

If they bang porn off the internet
All those love hungry fantasists
Will start having bad ideas
And most likely go into politics
If they bang porn off the internet
Kinky Stella N Roxy Rosie
Will be working in your local pub
Queefing on the pint heads N spitting in your grub
Keep the wankers in their bedrooms
And the whores on all fours
Seen only by the camera lens
Behind closed doors
Keep the institution going
For the needy N the frigid
I don't wanna find a couple shagging on my doorstep
Keep porn on the internet

BOULEVARD OF THE RESTLESS

The estate of wooden windows
The playground of abandoned homes
In the theatre of complacency
Chalk love letters on cardboard walls
Where stranger's whispers cling
Like blood seeping into a bandage
The air tainted by smoke rings
And words meant to cause damage

In the residential loony bin
In the centre of the overfilled ashtray
Content with burning out
Through the headless familiar days
Where the rain remains constant
The bad mood never swings
Where optimism remains inclement
As the bluebirds refuse to sing

I can feel the world
Within the itching of my feet
I can hear its heart murmur
In the vacant street
This slow vibration
Bleeding into the consciousness
Of the short existence
That plagues all of us
Poverty leaves us blessed
On the boulevard of the restless

Along the uncertain frontier
In the places where nobody goes
All the locals remain invisible
As they choose to stay at home
Loitering in the forgotten district
Calculating an eazee way out
With the world falling away at our feet
In the unread manuscript night

Everyone is a silent member
To the club of the anonymous
Where childhood dies before it's time
And adulthood has too many issues
Painted insults on decaying structures
Neglected like the church
We seek for a shred of faith
But end up in the lurch

A sparkly mosaic
Won't alter this scene
No trough with flowers
Won't invigorate the sting
Of the familiar sadness
That greets us with the sunrise
Swept under the carpet
As the lucky wait for us to die
No land to build upon
To make any difference
Everything remains derelict
And spared of expense
There's no solution
Or corners to cut
No eazee way out
Cos all the exits are shut
Lumbered with the disillusion
Of too much choice
So much to say
But left without a voice
Too much time
Only to be bored
No job, no money
No opportunities to score
Nothings legitimate
There's no clean slate
No place to trade
Or circumstance of fate
But we're connected
Whether we like it or not
Always wanting something we haven't got

Strung to the idle hands that play
On the boulevard of the restless

SUICIDE

British Gas will still remain in business
For when the last bottle is emptied
And a man feels no reason
For his existence
Windows closed
Oven on
Gas light flickering
Goodbye, so long
Death is a big money maker
As all of those disposable razors
Scratch away the life line
Of all the forgotten mover's N shakers
Deep bath
Door locked
Nerves chipped away
As blood mingles in the filthy tub
It's not a nice subject
But a man needs to think of these things
Sometimes
Just so the spectrum
Can be handled and one can smile
At something as simple as a blue sky
Christmas can sometimes be
Worth all the bullshit
If it shuffles off someone's
Mortal enemy
The fake trees
The consumption of consumerism
All those John Lewis adverts
Then someone forfeits their position
All those eazee little pills
To keep one calm
Can switch off all common sense
When there are no more dreams to kill
Another uncounted
Handful to relieve
The pain
Only to never wake from one's sleep

Nobody likes to talk about these things
Due to the severity N the force
That one can lose their way and life can turn ugly
Through a disheartening lack of choice

FANCY NAMES FOR SHIT JOBS

I need a title
To give my shit job meaning
Something that adds depth
To something so demeaning
I need a pseudonym
Cos I can't act me wage
I need an addition
To give my career a little extra added flair
House keeper is not adventurous enough
I prefer the term dust coordinator
Or a dead hair n loose skin technician
Even a feather duster terrorist would be preferred
Dishwasher holds no excitement
I'd rather be cared a fairy liquid chemist
Or a china plate stain inspector
Jay cloth Samaritan would give my role a twist
A box surgeon
An origami practitioner
A safety knife artiste
Or cardboard conqueror
Rather than bin man
Refer to me as a shit smuggler
Or a sultan of the dump
I'd even except Rubbish Undertaker
Eight hours of boredom
To keep a roof over me head
To keep me occupied
Until I wake up dead
The moneys a pittance
And the hours are too long
But it'd help to get through the day
If I had a fancy title for my shit job

NOWT BETTER

There's nowt better than that 1st wank in the morning as soon as the alarm rings
Nowt more effective than that 1st cigarette
Nowt more splenderous as the sound of the kettle reaches its boiling peak
Nowt head N shoulders above that 1st beer shit
To bring me back round
And reinvigorate my senses
To revitalise my heart
Only to realise that the night has ended

There's nowt greater than getting your favourite seat in the canteen
Nowt more exceptional than the weekly intake
There's never a better feeling to see the minutes rolling by
Nowt better than the seconds scratching their heads wondering why
To enliven the waning pulse
To update the operating system
To freshen N resuscitate
Your intrepid symptom

Nowt more suitable than getting home ten minutes earlier from yesterday
Nowt more fitting than the TV been interesting
Nowt kore exceeding when you realize the weekend is only 24 hours away
Now more fulfilling than the solitaire orgasm lasting
To renew a sense of purpose
To prompt the fire in your fortitude
To vivify N reanimate
The boldness of your ineptitude

Nowt better than sitting back after a long day's work
There's nothing more enriching living with the helpless and the depraved
Nowt more rewarding than winning a game of pool on a fluke
But nothings beats the 1st pint at the end of the day

DITZYLAND

Mickey needs a hit
Of brownstone locomotive
To turn his frown upside down
And ease his morning shits
Last giro cheque bounced
Owing too many favours
All are the droppers are empty
No more possessions to steal from his neighbours
With a permanent itch
On a diet of flea's N rizla's
To get his fix he gets on his knees
And swallows his dealers love paste

Daisy answered 'Yes'
To her sweetheart's proposal
De-evolving in caravan suburbia
With a litter of unwanted elders
Her 20 stone lothario
With his caffeine laced semen
Pumps her until the bed gives way
And she's left bleeding
She speaks when she's spoken to
And does as she's told
Has his dinner ready by five
Or else he romances her with his knuckles

Bursting into tears
Rather than into songs
Morals exchanged for tricks
And principles forgotten
Animated in monochrome
Just recycled animals
There are no happy endings
Down in Ditzyland

Donald works 12 hours a day
Fitting letters into envelopes
In fear of not reaching his targets

As he waits to go home
Back to his lettered room
Where the rats all linger
Counting away the seconds
On a hand of 3 fingers
Just another ghost
Who cannot articulate
The sense of detachment
From the rest of Fantasia

Minnie's an emotional cripple
From too many bad suitors
Hydrated by mother's ruin
As she tries to steal back her future
Goofy is split down the middle
Not sure if he's human or a dog
Ashamed to tell his wife N kids
That geezers named Tinkerbelle fuck him in the office bogs
All those happy little innocents
Faced with adult problems
Discover when they awake in the morning
That they are just another strain of whore's N villains

All the kings and queens
Of the industrial toon town
On a quest of sabotage
Until the sun goes down
Nightmares N suicides
With botched escape plans
There are no happy endings
Down in Ditzyland

OFFERS

A seventy-pound jumper
In fire damaged fashion
A new winter coat
Sold at a fraction
A car radio
That's just been lifted
A pair of trendy shoes
Without the laces
A reasonable priced I Pad
That turns out to be an etchasketch
Sold to the karaoke king
Who's now become a wreck
So many deals
How can I decline?
Surrounded by gentleman thieves
With deals of a lifetime
Ten quid
For a plethora of items
Jay cloths, feather dusters
And an undialled clothes iron
A 3-piece suit
Taken from a dead man
Cos the name brand
Didn't cover his funeral plan
HD movies
Downloaded by pirates
Sold from the back
Of a 3 wheeled wagon
A matter of life N death
For the bloke with the Lacoste T-shirt
And a brand new purse
Picked up on a 5 finger discount
A movie poster that doesn't stay on the wall
A pair of skid marked draws
A blowjob from a toothless Joe
These wondrous offers I cannot ignore

LOVE IS A BALL ACHE

Sally Cinnamon prefers the fairer sex
Molly ran off with Captain Farrell
Nancy called the pipes for Danny boy
After Rocky Raccoon was shot N killed
The angel in the centrefold turned out to be a mannequin
Mary Anne's hands only shook cos she was on the detox
The sad eyed lady of the lowlands never mustered a grin
And wicked Annabella's chastity belt has always been locked

Romeo bled out like a stuck pig
Dillinger was shot down by the lady in red
It may be all you need
But love is a ball ache

The unattainable woman on the hill in the long black veil
Remains a constant mystery to me just like sweet Jane
As Sharona remained forever young
As the drums continue to bang for Polly who got away
Rosie was just a whole lotta bad luck with mental health issues
Maggie McGill is a strange kind of wonderful
Ruby Tuesday came down with the Birmingham Blues
It's times like this I wish I'd fallen for a Jersey Girl

Quinlan was laid to waste in dirty water
Charlotte the Harlot rarely opened her legs
When all's said N done
Love is a ball ache

LETTERS

I write letters to the heavens
Hoping for a stroke of good luck
I write letters to the heavens
For a bag of cash N a girl to fuck
I write notes to the angels
Who are always on call
I pen scriptures to the dumb
Who've heard it all before
I pray for a continuous windfall
And a face that I can slap
For when my vision is consumed in red
And my good mood turns bad
I hope for resolution
And safety in the loyal
And the hatred of the behaviour of myself
When my blood begins to boil
I write letters to the heavens
In hope of some understanding
Not just lip synced connections
From those that never landed
From their self-righteous achievements
And binges of entitlement
Believing a shoulder to cry on
Brings forth enlightenment
I scratch notes to the saints
Who are not in session
One after the other over N over
As my straightjacket beckons
I scrawl notes to the seraphim's
Who are most likely getting plastered
I hope they are having a good time
As my pleas remain unanswered

UNIVERSAL TRANSMISSION

I was lost in the airwaves
Trapped in the static of the same old days
Waiting on the hard line
All the wild horses passing me by
Lost in the dream pipes
Searching for a way out every night

I want you to receive me
I want you to know the position I'm in
I want you to hear me
This is just another universal transmission

I've been biding my sweet time
Running round my head are the same old lies
That people have told me
But they never said of what I could be
I was waiting on the signal
Left by the ghosts that had their fill

I'm waiting for someone to respond
I'm waiting for a hand to hold
I'm waiting for a friend that won't go
I want to learn something I don't know

I want you to receive me
I want you to know everything I've been through
I want you to hear me
Just another universal transmission looking for you

FUCKTOBER

Two acceptable vices
To keep me socially active
One keeps me friendly
The others just another nasty habit
A pair of common affectations
Eradicating brain cells N lung tissue
A self-destructive operation
To quill the moldering issues
Immersed in restless lethargy
Chained to the disposable flame
Chemically overloaded internally
My senses routinely stained
12 steps to the public dispensary
And I become recklessly illuminated
Fumes locked to my unsteady breath
On a prescription of the sedated
Sustained on jailbird currency
Cursed with continuous dehydration
Docile N medicated
To escape the modern conscription
I need a sponsor
For the charity of myself
A spotter for the waste
Of my physical N mental health
A reprieve at the end of the day
Deteriorating from fermented broth
I'm unreachable in this escapism
Stoptober? Fuck off!
In the machinery of lonely evenings
With the unit orchestra in full swing
I swallow the amber river
And wheeze on permanent smoke rings
I have not yet begun to defile myself
I demand this finery to the end of humanity
Available from the unlocking of the shutters
This decadence is a permanent formality
Don't stop me now
Enough is never enough

Stoptober?
Fuck off!

CRANK

I hear a toilet flush
Every time I look at you
When that dingleberry blasts
At the bottom of me loo
I'm reminded of your grace
Your sense of style
Gets me right here
Just like bile
You give me fever
Like a chest infection
You speak with spelling mistakes
So that lessens the conversation
Like a flea loves its host
Like warts on genitals
Like shit sticks to a blanket
I can't get rid of you
You remind me of Nurse Ratchet
When she was nearly choked to death
Or when Tuco was strung up
By his scrawny neck
If I had the chance
Then I'd do the same
I'd piss on your grave
Or shove your ashes down the drain
I start to cringe
Whenever you call my name
You're crazier than a shithouse rat
You are certifiably insane
Like Oedipus loved his father
Like flies on a turd
Like the smell of TCP
You do nowt but disturb
My waning civility
You're someone I just can't fathom
I can't put my finger on it
Maybe you are the wrong sperm
That made it to the finish line
But doesn't cut the mustard

To call you human
Would be a clusterfuck of misappropriation
Like a badly timed fart
Like a chafing skid mark
This description suits you to a tee
CRANK!

FUCK THE CHEMIC

I spent 60 quid
In a space of four hours
Listening to poetry about politics
And shitty Springsteen covers
The landlady
Should've been a blowjob
But instead she's a crank
Who won't serve beer snobs
They close the curtains
To safeguard the regulars
Who dislike a challenge
And a new train of thought
As the bloke with the lute
Scratches his pubic beard
Thumbs a few notes
Then wonders why he's even here
Be prepared she's on the warpath
Cos you foolishly didn't place your pint on a beermat
As the knight on the sex offenders register
Throws a tray of empties
That miss her by an inch
Cos he's clotched once again
The music's too loud
It'll upset the neighbours
Serves em right for living
Next door to a public house
The taxi's late
We're stuck hanging about
Supping up N hoping
We'll be home by morning light
Then she storms out
All guns blazing
Claiming that we're pissed
And we need to start behaving
We've had too much
We've overstayed our welcome
Our mere appearance
Has caused utter bedlam

Like naughty school kids
We're sent on our way home
The end of the line
Is the title of this ode

ALTERNATE UNIVERSE

There's something rotten afoot
I can feel it in my brain fungi
My mind onions are tingling
There's something just not right
Lines have become blurred
Acceptance has clouded rationality
Ideals are now commodities
That are quickly dropped
At the first sign of trouble
When the shit hits the fan
You turn around to find
That you're an army of one
As the devils run amok
Good guys finish last
Normality shadows lunacy
Everything is overcast
Complacency holds integrity hostage
Evil holds its own satellite
That revolves around the separating plates
Leaving us stranded
Joy is stolen regularly
The bad guys always win
The wrong people get the bullet
Hope is just another rape victim
We live with changes
In which we have no say
We always miss the meeting
The memo never comes our way
We were told to live without fear
Now we're told 'DON'T TRY'
Love N peace became no pain no gain
We're uncaged birds with nowhere to fly
Perhaps in another galaxy
Another astral plain
In a stranger's fingernail
There is an alternative
The meek have inherited the earth
Loyalty N truth is rewarded

Love conquers all
But we're stuck in this alternate universe
Where we do what we can
Although it's not enough
We're simply resigned
To what we don't want
If we treated each other better
Then maybe our existence wouldn't be a waste
But in this alternate universe
No justice comes from this prayer

COMES N GOES

I can't quite remember what I'm doing here
If I had an agenda
Then its disappeared
No one gives a damn that's perfectly clear
It comes N goes
Over the years

I've tried and failed so many times
From here and there to back again
Seems whatever I'm reaching
Will have no end
It comes N goes
Over N over again

We don't speak the same language
We don't share the same tongue
Whatever I used to be
Is now dead N gone
It comes N goes
Just like the sun

The same old situations
In the sitcom of life
Same old conversations
Perfectly timed
In comes N goes
With the wheel of time

I've had my fill
Of the same old thing
I've had enough
But I won't give in
It comes N goes
Like the songs I sing

Just for a little while
Until the rains gone away
Hold my hand

So I know that you are there
It comes N goes
There's nothing left to say

WEIRD N WONDERFUL

Tuneful suitcases
Whistling at the Queen
Iron stallions
Half-heartedly grazing
Ulcers rumble
The sky grumbles
As we welcome the rain

The phantoms of Eden
With composite syringes
Papier mache organs
Dancing on cardboard ledges
Teeth lost in the snow
Surrounded by distant echoes
Of a world beyond the brink

Tender nothings kill
Amyl sniffer chills
Everything unfolds
Right on schedule
Oh so beautiful
All too weird N wonderful

Red eyed organ grinders
Scoffing bruised fruit
Barbed wire banquets
With anaemic roots
In the acclimatized upheaval
The soft touch of evil
Becomes a fatal shove

On shorthand bathroom tiles
Spooky little riddles
Topographic paddling
In dirty puddles
In the opiate sentinel
Where everything remains still
Stone age lovers tremble

Shoulder to shoulder
With the angels
In the festival
Of failed endeavours
Oh so beautiful
All too wicked N wonderful

NO ACCESS

Discount primetime media thrills
Pseudo electric psychobabble
Grotesque N wonderful
Monopolised syndromes of the subliminal
Fractured visor perception
Except the dance of the cadaver
Second hand pantomime ordeals
Spellbound ricochet stargazing
Corporate levers manipulated
Adventures in sepia widescreen
Intense N seminal
All the street celebrities have emigrated
Planning the inscriptions on their tombstones
Disenfranchised jumpsuit mania
We're still alive so eternity must have us
Spirituality is a cause worth fundraising
Footsteps pacing in empty rooms
Storm trooping in hobnail statements
The siren awakes from duvet thunder
Wishes drowning in black ice concoctions

Pavement sky
My footprints on the wall
No access past this point
Nothing happens at all

Sweet seraphim with a dirty glass
Listen to the children speak with severed tongues
As the anvil of the dawn crashes down
And the seekers all wait for their turn
News room clinical manifestos
Heated leopard skin protests
Distorted machine gun acoustics
Riots of the anesthetised soul
Cataclysmic ordeals by the minute
Clinging to the superstitious paradox
Hope rests on the sound of the alarm clock
Tied to the prospect of an extra life

Devious contracts scrutinised
Manipulated spirituality
Face your own state of reality
Don't be another flat line jive bunny
Mad cries scattered on notice boards
Mutes destroy the silence with wagging tongues
Corrosive bullets in vitamin stimulants
If only we could get away from here

Pavement sky
My footprints on the wall
No access past this point
Nothing happens at all

FOR YOUR THIGHS ONLY

You make me vast N bulbous
I can barely contain my trousers
You fatten my tulip like no other
I even like the bruises you leave on me knackers
When the 3rd leg has flatlined
And the fear of impotency sets in
I only need to think of you
And I'm hard once again
I'm an immature ejaculator
Who'll tickle your belly button from the inside
My bell will ring at the back of your throat
As you recount all of the ceiling tiles

My love knows no bounds
There's nothing I can do
I'm for your thighs only
You lucky lady you

The smell of fish on me bedsheets
Is a welcome reminder
Of that glorious night
That you made the bedroom windows shatter
I was born to pump you
And lead you into disability
Cos when I'm through with you
You won't be able to walk properly
You make my trouser snake rattle
Because of you me pubes stand on end
You put Goosebumps on me man lumps
When people wonder why I slouch I tell them you're the reason

You stimulate my purple onion
You've really got a hold on me dowsing rod
I'm for your thighs only
Now get your kit off

MY MIDDLE FINGER SALUTES YOU

An outcast to the unsociable
A stranger to the weirdos
Draws phallic symbols on beermats
And wears his cap indoors
The 5th member of a 4 seater taxi
Always after a free pint
Just another fragile snowflake
Who should wear a sign that says: Hello I'm a fucking idiot
A loner to the isolated
Dyslexic, autistic master of every condition
Spouts out the word 'Retard'
At mental health organisations
Asks to borrow a quid
To get another drink
You turn him down
And he asks for a fiver instead
Brings his own booze
To the places he's been clotched
Sits away in the back
Hoping not to be clocked
By the bar staff
Who use his screenshot as a dartboard
As he throws his toys out of his pram
Accusing everyone of been a paedo
He'd tab a fag off the Marlboro man
And steal a sandwich from an Ethiopian
It's a such a shame
That his mother didn't swallow him
My middle finger salutes you
Now fucking do one

SPACE RAIDERS

Cloudy Swill burning a hole in my stomach
From too many pints and laxative cigarettes
I need bulk to level my insides
As I sigh upon realizing that they've run out of pork pies
What crisps have you got?
I drunkenly enquire
As me guts groan
Like a death metal choir
There's Deep Friend Cajun Squirrel
Flame grilled possum with ginger spice
I'd be happy with Ready Salted
Rather than Dorset Cream N fusions of Rice
What happened to Salt N Vinegar?
These new concoctions blag me head
Is too much to ask for a bag of Space Raiders instead?
Culinary fusions for 3 quid a bag
When all I want is a little snack
Nothing fancy, nothing debonair
20% crisp 80% air
Peaking duck with hoisin sauce
Is far too much for me
I want something eazee
But I'm accused of been 'too fussy'
Saurted Donkey N Deli Sensations
Make me feel sick
As I consider popping to the offy
For some Frazzles or Chipsticks
These new-fangled delicacies
Can't appetize my needs
I'm a simple man with simple taste
Can I just have a bag of Space Raiders please?

HEADLINES FROM THE BLACKHOLE

Ink on my thumbs
From collected tragedies
Stories of the mighty one
Abandoned in electric dreams
Imitations of the bard
As the equator sings
In the tropics of espionage
Where the underdog wins
Breakfast at Rosencrantz
With Guildenstern in toe
With Vladimir N estragon
Discussing mankind's woe
In the rat trap of desire
With the streetcars out of gas
In search of epiphanies
Forever clawing at the past

As the chameleon in protest
Says that all poetry has died
Only to realise that no one gave a shit
For prophecies N bad vibes
Musical wordplay
From a lonely room
Soaked in the rhythm
Of blood N woe
Tomorrow's supertramps pillow
Headlines from the blackhole

Mary Lou N her sailor boy
Asking questions to the dust
As Macmurphy N Moriarty
Hope aboard the magic bus
The in the libraries of the dunces
With dry manuscript hearts
In the silent confederacy
Of manifested stars
Time flies tomorrow
For the angels in the castle

Within the budding slaughterhouse
Looking for a piece of ass
Deep in the footnotes
In the narrative of self-will
Submerged 20,000 leagues
Waiting for the kill

Playing the beatnik title role
On the empty coffee shops
Something good must be happening
Cos I can hear the cops
Musical wordplay
From a lonely room
Soaked in the rhythm
Of blood N woe
Tomorrow's supertramps pillow
Headlines from the blackhole

Printed in Great Britain
by Amazon

22835590R00109